"Are those bullets? Are we being shot at?"

"Yes." Preston slammed the door to the smaller room and barricaded it with a chair under the knob. "Get online and contact the police. I'm going to keep the shooter away from you."

Holly logged into the internet from a kneeling position.

"9-1-1. What is your emergency?" The voice echoed over computer speakers.

"We are being shot at."

We? Did she just say "we"? Preston craned his neck around to send her a warning look.

Holly covered her mouth, eyes wide.

"Have you been shot?" the voice asked.

"No. No. The door is locked. I'm inside the computer room at Cedar Glen Lodge."

"Police are on their way. Has anyone else been shot?"

Preston splayed his hands as if getting arrested. Unless Holly did some quick damage control, he'd soon be in handcuffs.

Or he'd be dead.

The door vibrated as a body slammed into the other side.

Angela Ruth Strong sold her first article to a national magazine while still in high school and went on to study journalism at the University of Oregon. Her debut novel came out in 2010, and she's won both the Idaho Top Author and Cascade Awards for her work. She lives with her hubby and three teenagers in Idaho, where she also started IDAhope Writers to encourage other aspiring authors.

Books by Angela Ruth Strong

Love Inspired Suspense

Presumed Dead

PRESUMED DEAD

ANGELA RUTH STRONG

H HARLEQUIN® LOVE INSPIRED® SUSPENSE

Recycling programs
for this product may
not exist in your area.

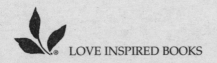 LOVE INSPIRED BOOKS

ISBN-13: 978-0-373-45691-8

Presumed Dead

Copyright © 2017 by Angela Ruth Strong

www.Harlequin.com

Printed in U.S.A.

I am come that they might have life,
and that they might have it more abundantly.
—John 10:10

Dedicated to Johnathan, Ashley and Kristina—
your creativity inspires me.

ONE

Preston Tyler lowered his feet from the deck railing and leaned forward as his gaze followed the Jeep pulling up next to the Fontaines' cabin across the lake. Though he'd been forced to hide out in his own family cabin for four years since being pronounced "dead" by the military, nobody had stayed at his childhood sweetheart's cabin at all.

Of course, he'd heard Holly had just canceled her wedding to Caleb Brooks. Maybe she needed a place to heal.

Preston should have considered the possibility and gone camping at Yosemite or headed to San Francisco to catch a Giants game. Honestly, a vacation in the Tenderloin District would have been better than seeing the woman he'd once loved mourn the loss of another man.

So, he wouldn't look. Preston inhaled deeply as he stood. Well, maybe he'd take one peek to see if it was even her. And if it was, he'd head inside until she left.

A lanky male frame climbed out of the driver's seat of the Jeep. Holly's dad? Brother?

Preston ignored the traitorous twinge of disappointment. It was better this way. Unless her family was getting the cabin ready for her arrival...

He squinted against the blinding sun for a better look at the figure pulling luggage out of the rear gate on the navy blue Jeep Cherokee. Only one duffel bag, but the man left the back gate of the Jeep open as he focused on carrying it to the house.

A warning alarm rang in Preston's head. He grabbed the binoculars he usually used when scouting for fish.

The dark man with a goatee retrieved a key from the top of the doorframe and looked around before cracking the door open. Not right. He wasn't a Fontaine.

Preston tracked the man's movement through the windows. There. In the bedroom. The stranger unzipped the duffel, looked at his watch and pressed a few buttons on a device that resembled an alarm clock.

Preston's guts churned. He'd seen bombs before, but only in the military, never in a vacation home. Why would anybody want to blow up an old cabin? Should he call the police with an anonymous tip? Or was he imagining things?

The man ran back through the house, replaced the key, slammed the rear gate of his Jeep and jumped into the driver's seat. Not good.

Preston ran a hand through his hair. He shouldn't have been involved at all. But just because he was supposed to be dead didn't mean he didn't care about Holly's family anymore. It meant he had to be discreet.

He lifted the binoculars again to get the license plate number of the SUV. Another vehicle crossed its path, blocking the license plate from view. Another vehicle? Headed toward the cabin? Preston raised the binoculars higher to get a look at the driver.

Holly.

She didn't turn or respond as the other car passed. She must not have known the man or been expecting a package. Could the stranger have set a bomb for her?

Preston's mind whirled with possible scenarios. Some

ridiculous. Some disastrous. But the worst scenario would be the one where he stood by and watched while someone else got hurt. He'd made that mistake before.

No matter how badly he wanted to shake the dread that gripped his heart, he couldn't deny the fact Holly's life might be in danger. He'd have to jump onto his parents' old Jet Ski and race what he suspected was a bomb. Keeping his life a secret wasn't worth risking hers.

Preston dropped the binoculars and grabbed his keys. Adrenaline surged.

Maybe she wouldn't recognize him after four years. Maybe she wouldn't believe it was even him. Or maybe she'd be too traumatized by the coming explosion to get a good look at his face.

If he reached the cabin in time to save her.

Holly Fontaine kicked her shoes off and padded barefoot down the warm, smooth dock. As a child, she'd always dived right into the lake, but as a woman—specifically, a woman scorned—she had other plans.

She pulled the sparkling engagement ring from her pocket. What had she been thinking, accepting the gaudy thing in the first place? It wasn't even her style. Caleb had insisted he'd paid a fortune for it and she deserved it. She'd made the mistake of listening to all her friends, who were so easily charmed by his expensive taste in jewelry, perfect smile and quick wink. They'd told her she wouldn't ever heal from a past heartbreak if she didn't move on. Now she had a second scar. Only this one wasn't in her heart. It was from the knife in her back.

At least she'd come to a good place to heal. Though coming alone felt more like punishment than anything else. But how else was she going to learn to reconnect with God? He was the One she should have asked about

Caleb in the first place rather than just assuming she was being given a second chance at love.

"You're enough for me, Lord," she said aloud. But did she believe it?

The smooth metal circle pinched between thumb and forefinger had offered promise. The promise of strong arms to hold her, as well as the promise of babies she could hold in her arms. A family. A place to belong. Now she was alone again.

She looked past the glittering diamond to the reflection of the sun off the water. Lake Tahoe brought back so many memories. Cliff diving. Capture the flag on Fannette Island. Fishing from Preston's canoe.

Holly ran a hand through her new pixie haircut and sighed. Reminiscence was supposed to get her thoughts off the current pain, but instead it intensified the ache. Why was it that the good guys like Preston Tyler died serving their country while jerks like Caleb Brooks got to live it up?

She was done thinking about Caleb. She had to move on with her life. Again. And that meant getting rid of the ring.

Caleb had said he didn't want it back, and she certainly didn't want anything to do with it. Maybe in the future it would wash up onshore and become someone else's symbol of commitment. Until then, it was her reminder of rejection.

Taking a deep breath of fresh mountain air, Holly cocked her arm and hurled the offensive piece of jewelry as far away as she could. It disappeared in the distance, and she didn't even get the satisfaction of hearing it plink into the water over the roar of a Jet Ski.

Oh well. She'd done what she should have a long time ago. It was better to be alone than to be with someone who didn't really love her. Even if it didn't feel better.

The dock rocked beneath her feet from the WaveRunner heading her direction. Time to get back to solid ground. Though she couldn't help being a little envious of the driver on the watercraft. So carefree. Able to enjoy the beauty of nature without worry. Escaping the pressures of reality.

She cast a longing gaze toward the person serving as a reminder of the kind of life she used to live. Another sad memory. Except…

She narrowed her eyes. Tilted her head.

Her crazy state of mind played tricks on her emotions. As if the memories weren't bad enough. But she couldn't look away. Couldn't stop studying the man who reminded her a bit of someone from her past. Take off those honey-colored sideburns and the stubble… Shrink the muscles a bit… Erase the frown lines in his forehead…

She had to stop staring. Because now the man was staring straight back. Intensity flashed in his familiar blue eyes. His lips parted. He called her name.

He called her name?

Holly shook her head. She had to be imagining things.

She willed the watercraft to rocket past. To prove her hallucination wrong. To leave her alone with her irrational daydream.

The Jet Ski slowed, sputtered, splashed cold water over her toes. The man on it extended his hand.

The last time this had happened, she'd been twenty-four. Headed back to law school for one more year while a younger version of the man in front of her prepared for his fateful promotion as a helicopter pilot in SOAR—Special Operations Aviation Regiment.

"No." This wasn't Preston. It couldn't be. Preston was dead.

"Get on, Holly. Now." The voice tugged at the strings

she'd used to sew her heart back together when Preston's charred remains came home in a coffin.

She had to be dreaming. She pinched her leg to wake herself up.

Ouch. Her thigh stung where she'd squeezed.

The man wrapped his fingers around her wrist and pulled her toward the Jet Ski. "This is real."

Real what? A real kidnapping?

"Who are you?" Her voice rose in panic.

She couldn't just climb on behind a stranger. If he didn't look so much like Preston, she would have pushed him off the watercraft by now.

"It's me, Holly."

Her mind whirled, almost pulling her head back with the weight of her thoughts. Preston was alive. He was on Lake Tahoe in front of her.

She covered her mouth with her free hand. This was impossible. Unless the corpse in the coffin had belonged to someone else and Preston had recently been released from some kind of POW camp.

She scanned his body, looking for injuries. If she climbed onto the Jet Ski too fast, would she hurt him? This was so unbelievable.

He tugged her arm. "Hurry, doll."

Her heart reeled at the old nickname. This was Preston all right. In a daze, she slid behind him and clutched both arms around his middle. He was more solid than she remembered. At least he hadn't been malnourished.

He gunned the engine. The Jet Ski tipped backward as it took off. Just like old times—

Except for the loud blast that erupted behind her. Hot air warmed her skin. Pushed against her. She craned her neck around to see fire shoot into the sky from her family cabin.

Her throat went dry. She clutched Preston tighter. If he hadn't just picked her up, she would be dead. But why? And how had he known?

Preston exhaled. He'd picked her up just in time. Though the sooner he dropped her off, the better.

He hadn't wanted to be right about the time bomb, but at least she was safe. He'd just have to make sure she was out of harm's way before handing her over to police. Because she had a life to rebuild, and he couldn't be part of it.

He slowed at his parents' old, weathered dock. He wouldn't have brought her here if they had been safe staying out in the open. But apparently someone wanted to kill her.

Her trembling fingers slid from around his waist to his sides as she twisted to look behind them. Her fingernails bit through his T-shirt. "What? What happened? What's going on? I...I don't understand." She looked at his cabin then at him, her eyes still too glazed to be afraid. "Why are we here?"

Preston viewed the dilapidated A-frame from her perspective. How would she react when she found out he'd been living there the whole time she thought he'd been dead? How much should he tell her? Had he just saved her life, or had he put her in even more danger?

She blinked. "I don't know what's going on. I don't know what to do. What do I do?"

Since someone was after her, he'd get her out of the open. Later, he'd worry more about finding the criminal. "Let's go in."

She climbed onto the dock, causing it to sink halfway underwater.

He eyed her ten pink toenails. So feminine. So sweet.

So off-limits. He forced himself to focus on hooking the towrope to the dock.

"I can't believe it's really you."

She gripped his biceps when he stood, and maybe she just saw him as her old friend whose shoulders she used to sit on when playing chicken in the lake, but her proximity wasn't as comfortable as it used to be. In fact, it was almost painful. It should be avoided because she wasn't even supposed to see him, let alone touch him. He stepped around her.

She turned, her arms flailing now that she wasn't hanging on to him like an anchor. "My cabin exploded. I could have been dead like you're supposed to be." She covered her mouth with her hands. "I can't believe I said that."

"It's okay." Though, was it? How was she going to explain surviving the explosion without revealing his existence? Was she even capable of keeping secrets?

She stepped forward. He stepped back.

"I didn't want to believe you died, but we had a funeral for you. They played taps and gave your parents a flag."

Preston looked away. He already knew about his funeral. He'd been there in the distance, watching, as his family mourned their loss.

Soon he would have to disappear again. No use giving Holly more to mourn. He'd put distance between them and a perimeter of defense around his heart. He wouldn't think about the first time he'd kissed her, at the age of sixteen under this very dock during a game of hide-and-seek. Or about how she smelled of coconut, the same way she had as a teen. He held his breath and stepped away, toward the cabin.

He had to concentrate on the danger of their situation. He'd trained for that. He looked back at the fireball that had once been her family cabin to make sure nobody had followed them across the lake.

She grabbed his hand.

Even though they'd grown up holding hands, his pulse reacted violently as an adult. The whole fight-or-flight syndrome. He'd be better off if he chose flight rather than to fight for a relationship that could never last. Dead men didn't date.

He led her along the uneven planks, up onto the deck and through the sliding glass door. His parents hadn't used the place since his "passing" either. Apparently both families had too many memories at the lake for them to be able to enjoy vacations there without him.

"How did you escape? Can I be there when you tell your parents you're alive?"

Uh…no. He took another step away and held up his hands so she couldn't follow.

She scanned him up and down. "Are you hurt? Were you held hostage? Who is after you?"

He lifted his eyebrows. She thought *he* was the target of the bomb? This was going to be worse than he'd expected.

"Holly." What a softer man he would be if he'd spent the last four years with her. Unfortunately, his current circumstances didn't allow for softness. "The bomb was meant for you."

Her spine shot straight. Her eyes snapped wide. She stumbled backward.

He stepped forward to stabilize her before she lost her balance.

She scampered away. "If the bomb was for me, how did you know about it?"

He held his ground. Tilted his head toward the deck. "I saw it being delivered."

Her gaze ricocheted back and forth between his eyes.

"How? Why are you here? Why does nobody know you're alive?"

He pressed his lips together. The truth was going to hurt. Just not as bad as the explosion would have. "I've been in the US for the past four years. I wasn't in the helicopter crash. I'd seen someone tampering with the engines and went to ask my sergeant to delay the op, but before he could halt takeoff, my team headed out. They didn't make it far before crashing into a fuel tanker. Someone else's body came home in my coffin."

She rocked onto her heels, gripping the back of the couch for balance. "You've been *pretending* to be dead?"

Was that all she'd heard? "Yes, because—"

"I am so tired of hearing men's excuses." Her hand covered her heart. Her voice lowered to a whisper. "I thought you were different, Preston. You used to be."

He held out his hands and blinked. What just happened? "You'd rather I be dead?"

"No." She took a couple deep breaths. Her eyes grew shiny, like she was about to cry—to mourn his death a second time. "I'd rather you tell the truth."

This was what he got for saving her life? A guilt trip? Of course, Holly didn't know he already had enough guilt to keep him from being able to return home. Probably forever.

But as for telling the truth, Preston had tried, and his sergeant had been killed because of it. SOAR Commander Robert Long had found Sergeant Beatty's body hanging in his bunk the morning after Beatty told Preston he'd look into possible sabotage. The death had been ruled a suicide.

Letting another person die because they knew the truth wasn't a risk Preston was willing to take, which was why Holly could never tell anyone about him, either.

"Holly, the CID—Criminal Investigation Division for

the military—hid the sabotage from the American people. They aren't going to let me come back to life and point fingers unless I know exactly who I'm pointing at, and I don't yet. So that means either the military will throw me in prison, or the person responsible for this will kill me. I have to stay dead for now."

He wasn't the bad guy here.

She shook her head. Shook it harder. "No. There has to be another way."

He used to think the same thing until it ate him up inside. "There's not."

But what-ifs still teased sometimes. What if Holly let the crime scene investigators back at the cabin presume *her* dead, and she started a new life with him off the grid? Or what if she helped him assume a new identity? Or what if he stayed in the cabin and she visited occasionally? Then he wouldn't be so alone anymore.

But none of those would be the best thing for her. He was there for her and not himself.

She planted her hands on her hips. "Am I just supposed to forget the way you popped back into my life today? Am I supposed to keep this a secret from your family, too? You know your little sister married my brother, right?"

"Holly." He couldn't help reaching for her.

She knocked his hand down. "That was supposed to be us. Don't you care?"

He folded his arms. He wouldn't tell her how he'd been glad at first when his old buddy Caleb looked out for her after his "death." Or how he'd broken a couple knuckles punching a tree when she'd finally said yes to the man's proposal. Or that he'd bought her an engagement ring before he left, and it sat in the loft above them collecting dust.

"I'm here because I care. I'm sure it would be easier

for you if you didn't know I was alive, but I saw some-one plant a bomb in your cabin, and I had to save you."

She glanced out the window. "Why would someone want to kill me?"

The question should rock him as well, but having played dead for the past few years, he'd found out more about murder than he'd ever wanted to know. "It could be a recently released prisoner whose case you lost. It could be a current criminal whose guilt you are about to expose in court. It could be a jealous coworker." Preston sighed. "Have you received any threats? Do you have any enemies?"

Her eyes rolled up to look at the ceiling as she thought, and Preston had a pretty good idea of who she was think-ing about. Finding her fiancé with the other woman had been an accident. Preston had simply planned to drop off a Bible and couple's devotional at Caleb's house as an anonymous wedding gift—a symbol to himself of wish-ing the best for Holly's marriage. But instead he'd stum-bled upon the fact Caleb was cheating. No way could he let Holly unknowingly form an alliance with a traitor, so he'd snapped a couple photos with his phone and stuck them in her mailbox. Of course, being a philanderer didn't mean the man was capable of murder...

"No. I don't think so." She looked to him, fear etched like stone in the gray depths of her gaze. "What do I do?"

Well, she couldn't die. He wouldn't let her. His family had already lost too much. She'd already lost too much. "I'm going to have to go back into hiding, Holly. But I'm here for you until I figure out who planted that bomb. You're going to be safe."

She stepped toward him. Probably wanting a hug for support, now that she was momentarily in the acceptance phase of shock. Whether it lasted or not, he couldn't be there for her like that. They would have to sever their connection soon, and it would be better if there was less to sever.

He grasped her hands to hold her at arm's distance. "You can trust me, but we can't be friends. I'll be leaving again, so I can't get close to you."

Footsteps thudded outside the front door. The doorknob rattled.

Preston didn't have any more time to worry about staying aloof. If he was going to consider himself a bodyguard, then he'd have to protect her. He wrapped one arm around her waist and dived behind the couch as the windowpane next to the door shattered.

TWO

Holly's muscles throbbed against the hardwood floor as the lock on the door clicked and the hinges squeaked. Someone was breaking into Preston's cabin. She held her breath, igniting fire in her lungs.

Footsteps thudded toward them, then stopped in the middle of the room.

She swallowed and looked at Preston to gauge his reaction. His blank expression hid all emotion, but his lack of fear gave her confidence. Did he have a gun? A knife? Experience in hand-to-hand combat? She'd thought she'd known him so well, yet this side of him was completely foreign to her.

He focused past her, looking underneath the couch. She turned her head to see what he saw.

Familiar tan leather boots. But probably just familiar because everybody wore outdoorsy boots in Tahoe. The kind of boots that would have no problem chasing her if she ran for the water or the woods. She'd head for the water. Being barefoot, she couldn't outrun the intruder. She'd have to outswim him.

The boots turned in a circle, as if the man were studying the small cabin. They tromped into the bathroom, then disappeared as he climbed up the ladder to check out the loft.

Had he gone all the way into the loft? Would she and Preston be able to sneak out without him seeing? She lifted her chin to visually measure the distance between her feet and the sliding glass door. If she could turn herself around, she might be able to slide the door open without making a sound.

But what if the rusty doorframe didn't cooperate? Or the intruder wasn't all the way up the ladder and he saw the door move? That was where Preston's military training would have to come in. Though if he had the survival skills she imagined he had, he should be the one planning their escape. She didn't know what she was doing.

She sent him a look of panic.

His fingers found hers. Gently squeezed. As if that was supposed to be comforting.

Did he know who had broken in? Did he know why? He'd said he had enemies of his own. Was this guy after him or her?

Help, Lord.

A phone jingled.

She jolted at the sound, clutching Preston's hand like a stress ball. Okay, now she was glad he'd made the connection.

Where was the noise coming from? Maybe she should let him go to silence the cell phone in case it was about to give away their hiding place. If it did, he'd definitely need his hand free so he could leap up and pop the bad guy in the jaw.

She uncurled her fingers and retracted her arm to give him room to fight.

The phone jingled again, the sound growing louder. But at least it was on the other side of the couch.

Preston shook his head. Not his phone?

"Yeah?" A gruff voice demanded.

Holly froze. Who answered their phone in the middle of breaking and entering? And had she heard that voice before?

"The woman got away on a Jet Ski."

Holly bit her lip to keep from gasping. This had to be the bomber. And he was talking about her. Had someone hired him to kill her? Someone like her ex's new girl-friend?

"Yeah, I'm sure. A guy just showed up at her dock and took her to another cabin. I had to drive to get here, and it looks like they've already left. No car in the driveway."

She searched for Preston's eyes. He'd just gone from being dead to being "a guy." This could mean trouble for both of them. But at least the bomber didn't know they were still in the room.

Preston squinted toward the direction of the phone con-versation as if it took all his concentration to make out the words.

"I'm inside the cabin."

Pause.

"I broke in through a window."

In place of the silence, a muted but angry voice yelled something in return. Could Preston tell if it was a man or woman on the phone? Because she couldn't.

"Well, since I'm already here, I'll just plant another bomb."

Another bomb? Preston's cabin was going to be de-stroyed the way hers had been? All out of a jealous rage?

Her fingernails bit into the flesh of her palm. Maybe Preston wouldn't have to fight the bomber after all. She was angry enough to take him.

More jumbled yelling.

"I won't use a *time* bomb again."

What other kinds of bombs were there? Holly had seen electronic detonators in movies. Or there were car bombs that ignited when the key was turned. Then there were the terrorists who strapped bombs to themselves. But it was ridiculous for Caleb's new girlfriend to send someone after her with a bomb. She was the only person Holly could think of who would be after her. Preston had mentioned a few other reasons someone might want her dead, but they all seemed so abstract.

Her skin grew slick with a cold sweat. She shivered.

"No more bombs? Fine."

Holly closed her eyes. *Thank You, Jesus.*

"Yes. I can do that. I'm on my way."

Holly watched the tan boots pivot toward the door. Her skin itched in anticipation of the man's departure. Was he moving in slow motion, or did it just feel like it?

Finally his feet stomped out onto the front step. The door snapped shut behind him.

She could breathe again. Her muscles melted toward the floor like snow tracked into the cabin in winter.

Preston's muscles sprang into action. He leaped from behind the couch and raced toward the shattered window. He needed to know for sure if the intruder was the same perp he'd seen at Holly's house.

A dark, lanky man climbed behind the wheel of a Jeep Cherokee. Same guy. What had Holly gotten herself into?

The engine revved. The SUV pulled away.

Preston grabbed a pen and scribbled down what he could catch of the license plate number before the vehicle disappeared into the trees. Because there was no way he was going to keep playing hide-and-seek with Holly. The Jeep's driver needed to be locked behind bars. That was the only way to keep Holly safe. Preston could find somewhere else to hide out if needed.

"Did you know him?" he asked Holly. She hadn't seemed to recognize the man when she'd passed him on the road earlier, but that was a completely different situation from being in the same room with him and overhearing a conversation about killing her.

"I...I don't think so." Her feet flopped out to the sides behind the couch. Apparently she wasn't planning to get up anytime soon. But they couldn't stay here.

He leaned over the back of the couch. "We've got to get you back to your cabin before the police think you died in the explosion. They'll find your car there and believe you were inside."

She sat up, eyes hard. "Why does it matter?" she challenged him. "You are letting everyone think *you* died."

He'd saved her life, and she wanted to argue? Of course, after finding out her fiancé cheated, her summer cabin blowing up and someone wanting her dead, it might be easier for her to focus on his problems rather than her own. Not that his were any easier to fix. But she obviously wouldn't understand unless she tried it out for herself. "You want to play dead, too?" he offered.

"No." She ignored his extended hand and grabbed on to the back of the couch to pull herself up. "I want you to *stop* playing dead so we can go talk to the police together."

"Let me know when you uncover the real saboteur, and I will be happy to go to police with you." She seemed to think he could reveal himself without causing any more death. In the best-case scenario of turning himself in, a lawyer much like her would pin sabotage on him and he would live the rest of his life in prison with no chance of ever finding the evidence needed to arrest the real criminals.

Since she didn't need his help, he climbed the ladder

into the loft to pack all the personal belongings he could fit into a drawstring bag.

"Okay," she said.

Okay what? He scanned the gathered items. It was a shame he didn't have time to haul it all down to the old pickup on the property at the end of the street. Hank, the older man who lived there, had started a new helicopter tour business and let Preston use his Chevy LUV in exchange for mechanic work. Unfortunately, the vehicle would probably have to be Preston's new home for a while.

"Okay, I'll find your saboteur."

Preston looked in her direction, but then had to step to the top of the ladder so Holly could feel the full intensity of his stare. "I was joking."

"I'm not." She stared right back.

Her determination was cute, but surely it would dissipate when she got back to the mess that was her own life. He scaled down the ladder rungs to lead her toward the sliding glass door so she could return to reality.

"One killer after you isn't enough?"

She stopped in front of him and lifted her chin. "All criminals deserve to be in jail. And it's my job to put them there."

It would be hard to do her job from the grave. Besides... "You're a defense attorney."

"Exactly. I'll defend you in court so the authorities can go after the real bad guys." She narrowed her eyes at his amusement. "You tell the world what you just told me, and I'll make sure they believe it."

He sighed. She had no idea how many times he'd considered such an option. But what would keep the same person who'd staged Sergeant Beatty's suicide from killing her? Or what if she lost the case and felt guilty that he had to spend the rest of his life in prison? He would never do that to her.

At least this way, everyone believed he'd died a hero. It was better for his family. And for Holly.

"I wish it were that easy," he said. Especially now that Holly knew he was alive and stood so close and cared so much.

She huffed and preceded him out the door. Nix on the "stood so close" part. And quite possibly the "cared so much" part.

He squeezed his fingers into fists. Too bad he didn't know the identity of the person who belonged at the end of his cross and uppercut. He'd settle for either the person who'd sabotaged his operation or the bomber who'd broken into his cabin. Or even Caleb. The man was an idiot for not protecting Holly the way he should have.

How many times would Preston have to give vengeance over to God? Always once more?

This is getting worse, Lord. He'd point out the obvious. Make sure God knew he still needed help. *Help me stay strong because I'm feeling pretty weak right now.*

His weak spot waited on the Jet Ski.

He shouldn't have even let her go out there alone. He needed to get her to the police as quickly as possible. She'd be safer with them than she was with him. He'd be safer, too.

He avoided looking at Holly directly as he joined her on the watercraft. And she held on to seat handles to avoid touching him as they made their way back across the lake. Or maybe she held on to the handles because he had the drawstring bag on his back.

Either way, God was giving him the help he'd needed. But it felt hollow somehow. Empty. Lonely. Though he should be used to that.

He cut the engine a few cabins down to stay out of sight of the emergency workers swarming the smoke-scented rubble. Turning halfway around, he spoke over his shoulder. "You're not going to tell police about me, are you?"

She bit her lip. "I will investigate the SOAR sabotage, but as that's not connected to this bombing, there's no reason for me to mention your existence to police today."

That would have to do for the moment. "Fair enough."

She lifted her eyes to his. "Where are you going from here? Don't you know anyone in the military who could help clear your name?"

Preston met her gaze. "I do have an old friend who used to be a JAG attorney."

Holly looked away. She wouldn't know he was already aware of her broken engagement, and she obviously didn't want to tell him about it. "I've got my bathing suit on underneath my jeans. I'll swim back to the cabin, and I'm sure investigators will never imagine I've been riding around on a Jet Ski with you."

"Thank you." He exhaled in relief. She may not be happy with the situation, but hey, neither was he. "Hopefully, they can figure out who set the bomb, and you won't need me anymore."

She searched his eyes before twisting away to pull her sweatshirt over her head.

"Tell the detective you passed a navy blue Jeep Cherokee with California plates as you pulled in. I didn't get the full plate number, but it starts with a 5AO."

"5AO," she repeated dutifully.

This wasn't how he'd imagined a reunion with her. But it wasn't really a reunion. He was only there to keep her safe. He focused on the scene she'd be heading back to. Fire engines sprayed water onto smoldering log remains. Police questioned neighbors. An array of boats slowed so passengers could rubberneck. A silver Jaguar pulled down the drive.

Preston's stomach warmed. His gaze swiveled toward Holly to see if she'd noticed the vehicle.

She scanned the beach as if in a daze, and he knew the moment her gaze hit the Jag. She dropped back down onto the seat behind him, but she didn't say anything.

If she didn't want to talk about it, he wouldn't mention Caleb's arrival, but he hadn't forgotten the man's presence. And there was no way he could let Holly spend time alone with her former fiancé on what should have been the weekend of their wedding. What if Caleb took her roller coaster of emotions for another ride?

"After you talk to the police, I want you to go stay at that lodge where our parents used to take us for barbecue ribs. I will come check on you."

No response.

Preston looked over his shoulder.

Holly watched Caleb park. It hurt to think that she'd gone from trying to help Preston to focusing on the other man so quickly. Even though Preston hadn't wanted her help in the first place. He'd wanted her to forget him so she could move on with her life. But the reality of it all stung like shrapnel.

"Holly?"

She blinked and turned to him, though her eyes remained distant.

He shouldn't blame her. She'd had quite a day. "Where are you going after you talk to the police?"

She stared. Maybe she hadn't heard him. Maybe she was going into shock. "Cedar Glen."

Good. He tilted his head toward the water, indicating it was time for her to dive in. The sooner she answered police questions, got rid of her ex and was safely at the lodge, the sooner he would be able to see her again. But that didn't make letting her go any easier.

THREE

Holly stumbled up the beach, her body trembling and dripping from the swim. She didn't want to talk to anybody. Especially not Caleb.

Preston's return had hit her like the force of water from a fire hose. And his dismissal had left her feeling much like the crumbling remnants of the cabin. Not to mention the attempts on her life.

"Holly." Caleb's brand-new, colorful hiking boots slipped in the gravel as he rushed to her with a fireman's blanket. "You're alive. Do you know what happened here? I was scared to death. How'd you escape?"

Holly tensed at his attention. She wasn't his to worry about anymore. "Calm down, Caleb. I'm fine." Fine. Ha. Who was she kidding?

"That is such a relief." He wrapped the scratchy blanket around her shivering shoulders, which would have been nice if he hadn't kept his arm around her, as well. "I'm just thankful you weren't in the cabin. Did you go swimming as soon as you got here?"

She shrugged out of his grip and ignored the question. But at least Caleb had been concerned for her welfare and was now acting thoughtful. She would have expected him to take off on their honeymoon with his new girlfriend.

"Thanks for the blanket." Her teeth chattered. It may be June, but the lake temperature only varied eight degrees from winter to summer.

Caleb tried to wrap his arms around her again.

She shook him off. Not happening. "What are you doing here?"

"The neighbors called your parents when the cabin exploded, and they called me to see if I knew where you were."

Holly eyed him. Mom must have been really worried about her if she'd asked Caleb for help. Though how had he gotten to her cabin so fast?

"I'm so thankful you weren't injured. I never got the chance to tell you how horrible I feel about what happened between us, Holly. It was a mistake. And actually I was planning to stay on my boat in hopes you'd call me so I could drive over here, and we might work this out." He gripped her hand. "Please."

She grimaced at his touch. There was nothing to work out. Particularly not now that the first man she'd ever loved had shown up alive again. As dishonest as Preston's death was, his presence reminded her how good they'd had it once upon a time. And Caleb was not once-upon-a-time material. She pulled away.

An officer with a receding hairline strode over. "You're Holly Fontaine? This is your cabin?"

"My parents own it." Good, a distraction. Except now she would have to answer a bunch of questions in a way that would somehow leave out Preston's existence. Maybe she should be the one asking the questions. She'd take on her attorney persona. "What happened?"

"Ma'am, I'm glad to see you survived. My name is Officer Shaw, and I hate to tell you this, but a bomb went off in your cabin earlier today."

"A bomb?" The idea still shook her.

"Yes, ma'am. Do you know of anyone who'd want to harm you?"

She looked at Caleb. Pretty convenient he just happened to be in the area. The bomber had been talking to someone on the phone. Could it have been him? No. It was more likely the other woman wanted her dead, now that Caleb seemed to want to make things work with Holly.

"What's your girlfriend's name?" she asked.

Caleb reeled. "No. That's ridiculous. She's not my girlfriend. And she wouldn't do this anyway."

Officer Shaw pulled his sunglasses lower on his pockmarked face to look at the other man. "I will check her alibi. What's her name?"

Caleb shifted his weight side to side. "Denise Amador. But make no mistake, she didn't do this."

Holly lifted her chin. "She obviously wasn't above having photos taken of you two together and sending them to me."

Caleb's voice lowered. "You still think she did that?"

The officer chewed at the fingernail on his thumb. "I'm going to need to interview you both separately."

Holly blew air into her cheeks. None of their old relationship stuff even mattered anymore now that Preston was in the picture. Because Preston was the only one who should have ever been in the picture—the old Preston anyway.

The old Preston never would have left her to talk to police by herself. The nickname "doll" came from the way his parents said he used to like to play with her as much as his little sister liked playing with her dolls. She smiled sadly at the memory. Preston had called her "doll" to get her on the Jet Ski, but not because he wanted to rekindle their friendship.

She focused on Shaw. "That's fine, Officer. I'm not planning to talk to Caleb anymore anyway."

"What? Why not?" Caleb held his hands out as a different cop motioned him away. "Is there another man in your life?"

No. Just the shadow of a man. "Goodbye, Caleb." Preston or no Preston, her main regret with the lawyer was that she hadn't said goodbye sooner.

Shaw led her toward the police car next to her totaled vehicle. Debris had smashed into it, and the heat had melted everything from her purse to her computer to her luggage. She'd need to go shopping, but could she even get money out of her bank without a license and debit card? Maybe Dad could wire her some cash for the rest of the weekend. She'd hole up at the lodge, waiting for Preston to show up again.

Or had she been knocked unconscious by the blast from the explosion and dreamed the whole Preston thing? That would actually make more sense than his sudden appearance after four years.

"What's your relationship with Mr. Brooks?"

Blech. Holly didn't want to even think about Caleb. Had he been cheating on her the whole time? "We were supposed to get married this weekend, but I found time-stamped pictures of him with someone else in my mailbox last week."

Officer Shaw scribbled notes. "You don't suspect Mr. Brooks set the bomb?"

She leaned back against the seat. "No. He obviously lacks morals, but he's not stupid."

The policeman gave her a hard look.

She shrugged. "We're defense attorneys. If he'd planted a bomb, he would have made sure he had an alibi far away from here."

Shaw scratched his head with the back of his pencil. "We will check out his alibi. You really think Ms. Amador would go to such lengths?"

Up until twelve days ago, Holly hadn't even known the woman existed. "I don't know." She thought back to Preston's suggestions that a former client might be after her. Would he have considered Denise a suspect had he known of Holly's broken engagement? It didn't matter now. The police were looking into it. She told Shaw about the blue Jeep before asking for a ride to Cedar Glen.

The resort had been remodeled since Preston's last visit. It was a nice change, though it made him sad how easily life went on without him. Holly probably wouldn't need him around for long, either. Hopefully, she'd kept her word and hadn't mentioned him to authorities.

She arrived a couple hours later in khaki shorts and a ruffled, baby blue tank top, carrying a shopping bag. Her parents must have wired her some money.

He waited until she'd checked into Cottage 19 before scanning the surroundings and knocking on her door. It would have been safer for her to be in the main lodge, but the place always booked up months in advance.

"Who is it?"

"Preston." Saying his own name sounded strange. He usually gave a different alias everywhere he went.

The door swung open. "So you are real. I thought maybe I'd imagined the whole thing." Holly left him at the door and sat on the brown leather sofa in front of a stone fireplace. She clicked the television remote to turn down the volume of the local news, which was covering the bombing she'd just escaped.

Preston closed the door and looked from the on-screen

reporter standing in front of the charred cabin remains to the woman whose great-grandparents had built it. "How are you doing?"

"Numb right now. My attorney brain is trying to make sense of all this, but the pieces don't fit together." She gave a wry smile. "Mom and Dad offered to drive up, but I told them you are taking good care of me."

His shoulders sagged until he registered her small smile. "No, you didn't."

Her smile disappeared. "I wanted to. I hate secrets."

"So do I." His secret was what kept him from taking her to The Rustic Lounge to enjoy a good meal and talking until midnight, the way they used to. "How did it go with the cops?"

The corners of her mouth curved down. "I might as well tell you about my cancelled engagement." She looked away. "My former fiancé—your old JAG friend Caleb Brooks—was at the cabin. Said he wanted to work it out with me. Police seemed to suspect him at first, but now they are looking into the other woman. I personally think she's more likely."

Preston clamped his jaw shut. He could get himself in trouble here if he wasn't careful. "I'd like to look into other possibilities."

She lifted an eyebrow. "You mean like check into which of my former clients have been released from jail recently and that kind of thing?"

"Yes." She'd be a good investigator with her experience in law and the research that went into it. Unfortunately, that was what gave her the idea she could help find his saboteur. He'd disappear before she ever got the chance to try.

She scooted over. "Are you going to sit down?"

He'd been planning to keep his distance. His mission was to find the person after her so she could return to her life safely. Nothing else. Which meant they had work to do.

"How about we go to the business office and use their computers for our research?"

She frowned. "You don't have a computer or phone?"

He shook his head. "I go to the library for research since I can't pay for internet or cellular service without a credit card."

Holly blinked. "Of course."

And hers would have been destroyed in the bomb blast. He tilted his head toward the door. "Come on."

Preston led her across the commons area with its picnic tables, fire pits and swimming pool, toward another small cottage structure that housed a few game tables in one room and computers in the other. Two kids swatted a Ping-Pong ball back and forth and didn't even notice them as they entered the smaller interior room.

Holly sank into a chair and ran an internet search on Operation Desert Hope before he could stop her. The black-and-white image of a burning helicopter took his breath away. It came to life in his memory with the roar of fire, the heat of flames, the smell of sulfur and the taste of acid in his throat. Shouts. Sirens. The realization he'd let his team down. Not to mention the failed recovery of hostages whose families counted on him to bring them home safely. Then there was Sergeant Beatty warning Preston to lie low until he discovered exactly what had happened.

Preston had failed them all.

"Holly." He pushed through the past to get back to the woman in the room with him. "We are investigating the bomb at your cabin, remember?"

She spun her chair to face him. "You're not giving up

on finding your saboteur, are you? Do you have any idea who it might be?"

His breath hitched. He couldn't do this now. "My first goal is to keep you alive. Please log in to your work files."

She narrowed her eyes. "Police are probably arresting Denise Amador right now."

Preston rubbed his temples. If she wanted to believe Denise was her only threat, how was he going to get her to help him figure out who the real enemy was?

Holly bit her lip. "Do you think Caleb will defend her? Nah. Never mind. I don't want to talk about him."

She didn't want to think about her situation at all. That must have been why she wanted to focus on him instead— why she was so adamant about investigating the helicopter crash.

"Holly, if you don't need my help anymore, I'm not going to stick around." He couldn't relive his last day with SOAR over and over, letting her hope she'd find something he missed. He knew what it felt like to have your hopes dashed, and he wasn't going to do that to her. If she refused to work with him to find out who was really after her, then he'd watch from a distance to make sure the police kept her safe and arrested the hit man and the person who'd hired him. That was probably the best thing for both of them.

She huffed but turned back toward the computer to log in to her files at work. "I'm going to look at this again later."

"Fine. For now, let's try to rule everyone else out before we focus on Denise," he suggested. Planting a bomb was not the logical next step up from stealing a boyfriend. "What cases have you lost in your career?"

Holly scanned the digital files. "Just a few. Dante Scott. The basketball player accidentally hit a kid who was running out in the street to catch up with a bus. Guilty of man-slaughter. The jury was just trying to make an example of him to all the other pro athletes who think they can get away with crimes."

Preston knew that case well, as did the entire country. It said a lot about her success in law that she'd represented the professional athlete.

He lowered into the seat next to her. "He got out of prison early for good behavior, didn't he? I'll look him up." The man's alibi would be easy enough to check. He couldn't go anywhere without the press following. "Next."

Holly scrolled down the list on the screen. "Madeline Carpenter claimed her twin committed the robbery, but we couldn't prove it. She's still in prison. You think she could hire someone to kill me from prison?"

"Possibly. We can check the inmate calling records to know for sure. Next."

"Taylor Everingham. He smuggled drugs over the border, but only because his wife's life was being threatened by a drug lord. They still found him guilty."

Preston leaned forward and gnawed on a fingernail. "Would he kill you if his wife's life was in jeopardy?"

Holly twisted a wispy strand of hair at the base of her neck. "Possibly. But he's still in jail, too." She leaned against her seat back, rubbing her hands together. "That's it. Do we go after Denise now?"

"We can. Or we can check out families of victims who were upset when you got a client off." Nothing rang true for him so far. There had to be someone more familiar with explosives. Someone with more of a motive.

"If that's what you want to research, we're going to be here all night." Holly tilted her head and smiled sweetly. "Can we go pick up some dinner first?"

Preston looked down to avoid smiling in return. She did not ask him out. She was asking him to feed her. Which was a good thing. If she'd been asking him out, he would have had to say no. "I'll call in an order of ribs."

She rested her elbow on the countertop and her chin on her fist. "Remember that time Dad was grilling ribs and a bear showed up, so we all had to hide out in the cabin, and dinner was burned to a crisp?"

Then their parents had brought them to Cedar Glen Lodge instead. "I remember. Bear or not, your dad always burned the barbecue."

Holly chuckled. "I think it's because he liked having an excuse to go out to eat so he could get out of dish duty."

Preston couldn't keep from smiling at her this time. He picked up the lodge phone to order from room service, as well as to distract himself from continuing down the path to memory lane. It took a moment for him to snap out of the past and realize there was no dial tone.

He pressed the receiver button a couple times. Still nothing.

The hair on the back of his neck stood on end. While he'd been reminiscing, someone had cut the phone line.

The lights remained on. The internet stayed connected. But if someone wanted to hurt Holly, Preston needed to get her out of there. Back to her cottage so she could call the police.

"Holly," he whispered as he rose. He motioned for her to follow him.

The game room stood empty now, which could be good or it could be bad. Good because he didn't want anyone else to get hurt. Bad because being in a public place might have kept *them* from getting hurt.

He scanned the area for a bomb. But a bomb wouldn't

warrant cutting phone lines. If there was really someone trying to kill Holly, the goal would be to get to Holly before she could get help.

She joined him. "What—"

He held a finger to her lips.

She frowned at him, then scanned the empty room. "What are we doing?" she whispered this time.

He couldn't look at her. Couldn't see the fear his words would cause. He'd be better off keeping his eyes open for the enemy. "The phone lines are down. We're going to get you back to your room, where you can call the police." As long as her room line still worked.

Holly's hands reached for his arm as she trailed after him. Fingernails dug through the sleeve of his sweatshirt. "You think someone still wants to kill me?"

That was what he'd been trying to tell her. Maybe now she would listen. He pressed her back into the wall beside the front door. He'd check their surroundings first, before they charged into the open.

She froze in place as he gripped the doorknob. Her fingers refused to let him go. That was fine. He wasn't going far.

He cracked the door open, squinting as the sinking sun momentarily blinded him. It was a gorgeous and peaceful day. Maybe he was being paranoid.

Pop.

Wood splintered next to his face from a slug.

He slammed the door closed. Twisted the flimsy little lock.

"What happened? What are you doing?"

Thankfully, the thick, log walls would keep out any more bullets. But the windows wouldn't. They couldn't keep people out, either.

Preston pried Holly's fingers off his arm. "Down. Crawl. Back to the computer room."

"Why? I don't under—"

Glass shattered from the window frame and tinkled to the tile floor.

Holly crouched and took off over the shards, toward the other side of the building. Preston followed.

The enemy wasn't holding back. An enemy that wanted Holly dead so badly they were willing to take out Preston in the process. Hopefully, there was only one shooter. And hopefully, whoever it was hadn't realized that the game room also included a computer room with internet access.

"Are those bullets? Are we being shot at?" she yelled back over her shoulder.

"Yes." He slammed the door to the smaller room and barricaded it with a chair under the knob. "Get online and contact the police. I'm going to keep the shooter away from you."

Holly logged in to the internet from a kneeling position. "I don't think it's Denise anymore," she said, trying to use logic to make sense of a life-and-death situation.

No. This was not a crime of passion. This was a premeditated attack. "I don't think so, either."

"911. What is your emergency?" The voice echoed over computer speakers.

"We are being shot at."

We? Did she just say "we"? Preston craned his neck around to send her a warning look.

Holly covered her mouth, eyes wide.

"Have you been shot?" the voice asked.

"No. No. The door is locked. I'm inside the computer room at Cedar Glen Lodge."

"Police are on their way. Has anyone been shot?"

Preston splayed his hands as if he could feel the handcuffs. Unless Holly did some quick damage control, he'd soon be wearing them soon.

Or he'd be dead.

The door vibrated as a body slammed into the other side.

FOUR

Holly's heart thumped as loudly as the thudding on the other side of the door. Would the chair keep the shooter out? As if having the same thought, Preston pressed his body against the door, as well.

Help, Lord. Maybe she should help. Adrenaline coursed through her veins, making her limbs feel strong and shaky at the same time. She dashed toward the door to keep the enemy out.

"Miss? Has anyone been shot?"

Oh, the emergency operator. She darted back. "No."

The door bulged again.

Holly's heart jumped. Would the enemy bust through? Would this be her last moment on Earth? Would her parents have to mourn her death the way they'd all mourned Preston? Her heart ached for them.

Preston anchored his shoulder against the wood. He pushed his feet against the ground. His red face scrunched with exertion.

Another bulge. The chair underneath the knob crashed to the ground. Space between door and frame grew larger.

Holly charged. Together they could push the door closed.

The barrel of a gun appeared, followed by a hand.

She dug her toes into the floor harder. Leaned forward. Reached for the door to smash the shooter's arm with the strength of her momentum. Almost there.

"Get down," Preston shouted.

Holly ducked, but kept on going. She could slam the door closed from the bottom as well as she could from the top.

Pop.

Her arm flew backward. Her ears rung like a firework had exploded in her face. She blinked, trying to figure out if she'd made it to the door or not.

Someone called her name in the distance. Tile rushed up to meet her. She reached to catch herself, but the moment her left hand touched the ground, a searing pain shot up her biceps. Or was that her triceps? The pain grew to overtake both areas.

Had she been shot?

Blood dripped down to her fingers. Her blood. She sank to the ground, feeling nothing but the mangling of her flesh. It radiated through her whole body. Made her dizzy.

Had Preston been shot, too? The weight of her eyelids pulled her eyes closed, so she couldn't find him. She tried to call for him but heard nothing except the low wail of sirens.

Police. Would law enforcement make it in time? Would she be okay? Would Preston?

Lord, please keep Preston safe.

Preston watched in horror as Holly sank to the ground. She'd been hit. It looked like a flesh wound. But still. He was there to keep her safe, and he'd failed.

With renewed strength, Preston pulled away from the door to ram his whole body back harder. The gun knocked against the wall. He'd caught the shooter's arm. Good.

Now the man couldn't aim anymore. To keep him there, Preston would have to wait for police to arrive, and he'd be caught as well, but at least Holly would be safe from whoever was trying to kill her.

Oh, God, don't let this guy get away.

Sirens rang in the distance. About time.

The gun thrashed in the shooter's hand as the man realized he was about to be caught. Preston pressed harder to keep the owner pinned in place.

The hand stilled. Was he giving up?

The door arched, sending Preston stumbling away. He reestablished his balance and charged back into position. The door slammed tightly into the doorframe. He'd given the man enough time to pull his arm out.

Preston's heart constricted. Not only had he let Holly get shot, but he'd let the shooter escape. He held his position until footsteps crunched over broken glass on their way out the front door. Then he lowered himself next to Holly and brushed a wisp of pale hair off her clammy forehead.

Sirens grew louder. Tires screeched. She'd be in good hands. Though the shooter had gotten away. Unless he chased the man down himself. Preston probably knew the area better than police.

"I'm sorry, Holly," he apologized quietly before sprinting out the door.

Darkness. Heaviness. Throbbing. Voices.

Holly opened her eyes. She was alive. In the computer room and surrounded by emergency workers. Where was Preston?

Her heart lurched. She used her good arm to press herself to a seated position and scanned the room. "Where is he?"

An EMT pushed her chest back toward the floor. She twisted out of his grip.

Officer Shaw strode over. "He got away for now, Miss Fontaine, but we'll find him."

They'd find Preston? Oh no. The policeman was talking about the shooter. Preston must have escaped before police arrived. He was okay.

She sank to the floor. *Thank You, Jesus.*

"Hold still, ma'am. I need to clean your wound." The EMT adjusted her arm with gloved hands and dabbed at the gash with some kind of cold liquid.

Holly gritted her teeth as the stinging increased. At least it looked better than it felt.

Shaw focused on her. "Glad you survived another attack. That was some quick thinking, using the internet to call for help."

Holly closed her eyes. She wouldn't have survived if not for Preston. Where had he gone? Would she ever see him again?

"So you propped the chair underneath the door and held off the gunman by yourself?"

Holly's eyes flew open. She hated dishonesty, and she wouldn't lie. She'd made that her policy from the very beginning of her law practice. But she'd also told Preston she would keep his existence a secret. *What now, Lord?* Her gaze zeroed in on a Bible most likely left at the lodge by the Gideons. That had to be a sign. God would want her to tell the truth.

"I wasn't alone."

Shaw followed her line of sight. "God was with you?" He harrumphed, then made a note in his notepad. "If there is a God who answers prayer, you're certainly keeping Him busy today."

Holly almost laughed. She'd been about to give Preston all the credit for rescuing her, but the policeman had thought she was talking about God. Maybe she should have been. God was the one who'd answered her prayers. He was the one who'd orchestrated events so Preston had seen the bomb being planted in her cabin earlier that day. God must have known this was going to happen back when they were kids. He'd brought them together to support each other.

Preston's friendship and commitment had gotten her through a lot. Like when she'd lost the freestyle race at the state swim meet. And when she hadn't gotten the scholarship to Stanford. And when she'd found out her best friend from high school had cancer. He'd been the one to suggest the polar plunge fund-raiser that had paid off Alexandria's medical bills from chemo.

Had she ever been there for him like that? He'd always been so strong and capable. But now he wasn't. He was nonexistent. And since she was the only one who knew he was still alive, she was the one who could offer him help.

The EMT dabbed her arm with gauze. "It's just a graze. I'll use some butterfly bandages to hold the wound together."

Holly cringed. She'd fainted over a mere scratch? At least she wouldn't have to go to the hospital and she could get her hands on a computer sooner to research Operation Desert Hope. Something bugged her about the online story she'd looked up. Something told her to look deeper. She just couldn't put her finger on it.

"Here, ma'am. I think this will help."

Holly waved away the pill and water cup. She just wanted these people to track down the bad guy and leave her alone. She had work to do. And she couldn't do it with a fuzzy brain.

Officer Shaw bit at a nail. "Miss Fontaine, this has to

be very scary for you. Until the person who did this is apprehended, I'm going to guard you around the clock."

Holly squeaked. And not just from the way the EMT pinched her skin together. She wanted the police to find out who was trying to kill her so she could move on with her life. Move on with helping Preston get his life back. She needed Shaw to leave so she could do that.

"How long do you think that will take?"

Officer Shaw studied her. "You've got somewhere else you need to be?"

The irony. On what was supposed to be the biggest weekend of her life, she had nowhere to go and nobody who would miss her. "All I have is canceled plans."

"I'm sorry, Miss Fontaine. This wasn't my plan for the weekend, either."

"Shaw." A short, redheaded woman in a business suit entered the overcrowded computer room carrying a clipboard. "We checked Brooks's alibi. He was down at the yacht club the whole time."

They still suspected Caleb? He could have been the voice on the phone, but since he'd never really loved her, having her cancel their wedding shouldn't have been that big a deal. Preston hadn't even suspected him. At least it was one more name they could cross off their list.

"It wasn't Brooks," Shaw stated. "Deputy Young saw the perp sneaking out a back window but lost him in the woods. Caucasian. Six feet, one hundred and eighty pounds. Tan with medium-blond hair and a camouflage hoodie. Knows the area really well, too. Put out an APB."

Holly gasped. Shaw had described Preston. He was after the wrong man.

Preston watched from up the mountain as the sun set and lights flicked on in the cabins below. He wiped sweat from his brow when an ambulance pulled away without Holly. She must be okay, but his stomach still churned at the idea she'd gotten hurt under his care. He wouldn't make that mistake again. She'd be better off with police protection. The same officer who'd been at the bombing now walked her across the commons to her cabin. Looked like he planned to personally guard her.

From now on, Preston would keep a safe distance as he watched for the shooter to return. The man had disappeared before Preston could follow him, but that wouldn't happen again.

If only they'd found a lead in Holly's work files. Maybe the police department would have better results than he'd had.

Cop cars pulled away from the scene of the crime one by one. A couple plainclothes detectives stuck around to record evidence. Had Holly been able to keep his existence a secret this time around?

Preston shook his head to free himself from the fear of being discovered. The more pressing issue would be to discover whoever was trying to hurt her.

Was he right in believing the shooter to be related to a client from her past? Or was it just a random psychopath? Or perhaps he should look into Denise Amador as Holly had suggested. The other woman could have hired a hit man. That could have been her on the phone with the bomber.

Preston rubbed his temples. Time to sneak down to Holly's cabin and wait outside a window for a chance to talk to her. He'd make sure she was okay after the bullet wound. And then he'd say goodbye. No matter how well they worked together or how good it was to see her again, his presence only complicated the situation.

After driving the old Chevy down the mountain and

parking on the street, Preston made his way to Holly's cabin. He hated having to leave her, and he hated *how much he hated* having to leave her.

He crouched down to avoid detection as he neared Cottage 19. He peeked through a window to find Officer Shaw in front of the television and Holly on the phone. Probably talking to her mom.

It had been years since Preston had talked to his own mom. The emptiness he'd once been used to now overwhelmed him like a tidal wave. Being with Holly, being known, had been a sip of water to a man in the desert. It wet his tongue, but made him realize how parched his throat had become. How would he survive if he had to head back out into the desert again?

Holly hung up. Spoke to Shaw. Turned toward the bathroom.

This was Preston's chance. He crept toward the light that flicked on through a frosted pane, swallowed down emotions and tapped on the glass.

Running water stopped. He tapped again. The sill trembled as she unlocked the window. It slid open silently.

Holly's face appeared. She squinted into the dark. "Preston? Oh, I prayed—"

He held a finger to his lips and pointed to the showerhead. She nodded, then disappeared for a moment. Pipes squeaked as the rush of water resumed. Now they could talk without being overheard.

She leaned toward him, her short blond hair illuminated like a halo from behind. "I'm so glad you're okay, but I have to tell you, I don't think I can keep your secret much longer. I almost revealed your existence to Officer Shaw earlier. And my mom knows something's up."

He'd requested she not tell police about him, but he hadn't figured in Holly's connection with her mother. And if Mrs. Fontaine found out, she would never be able to re-frain from spilling it to Preston's mom.

"I know it's difficult. That's why I have to disappear."

"What?" Too loud.

He held a finger to his lips again and tensed, waiting for Officer Shaw to come charging through the door. Sure enough. Footsteps.

"Miss Fontaine? Everything all right?"

Her glare told Preston she wanted to say no. "Yes, thank you," she answered anyway.

"Good. I'm going to step outside to call my wife, but don't worry, I'm not going far."

"Okay."

They waited for his footsteps to fade.

Holly rested a forearm on the sill to lower herself enough to look Preston straight in the eye. "You told me you would stick around until you knew I was okay."

He sighed. This wasn't an easy choice, and she wasn't making it easier. "You're safer with police, Holly. As much as I want to protect you, I'm just one man."

"Officer Shaw is just one man."

"He has a gun. And backup. You could have been killed today."

She searched his eyes through the steam floating from the shower. "When will I see you again?"

He started to shrug, but the gesture fell flat. This wasn't something he could shrug off. "After I figure out who sabotaged the helicopters."

She leaned forward. Did she want to kiss him goodbye? Like the last time he'd said goodbye? It had been differ-ent when he'd left for his tour overseas. They'd had hope for a future together. A kiss now would break through the walls that kept his heart from hurting. And yet the touch of her lips to his might be what brought healing and kept him going. It had been so long since he'd made any good memories.

Her hands clamped down on his shoulders. She leaned all her weight into him. Definitely not the most natural position for a goodbye kiss. He rocked forward.

Her face lowered toward his. She grunted. "I'm coming with you."

She hadn't been trying to kiss him after all. She wanted to use him for balance to climb through the window. Her torso already hung halfway out of the cottage. Why did she have to be so tenacious?

"No, you're not." He gripped her ribs to push her back in.

"Ouch." She pulled her injured arm to her chest.

He released her automatically to keep from hurting her any more. "You okay?"

"No, I'm not okay. You're the only one who really knows what I'm going through, and you're trying to leave."

He stepped closer to the window to push her back in. "For your own good."

She used his proximity to wrap her good arm around his neck. Was that the heat from the shower or her embrace that warmed his skin? "And for *your* good, I'm going to tell police everything."

His insides burned. After all he'd done for her, she was going to hand him over to go to prison?

"Holly, please." The whole world would turn on him. His parents would be harassed. That was, if they lived that long. Whoever had hanged Sergeant Beatty could also take out anyone else who might believe in Preston's innocence.

Her eyes softened. "Even if I try to keep it a secret, it's going to slip out. So take me with you. I can help prove you didn't sabotage the operation. I'm a defense attorney, and I'm really good at my job."

He wanted to believe she could help, but she was already in enough danger. He couldn't ask her to sacrifice her future. That had to be his burden alone. "Holly—"

A pinecone skittered across the ground toward them. Preston's muscles tensed. Was the shooter back? Had he just put Holly in the enemy's crosshairs?

The blue light from a cell phone floated around the side of the house, followed by muffled cursing. The communication device flew to the ground. Officer Shaw stepped forward into the light from the living room window, fumbling for his gun. "Stop!"

FIVE

Holly jumped at the sound of Shaw's voice, shifting more of her weight into Preston. The officer drew his weapon. Blood raced through her veins like a dam had burst. Preston didn't know the police had his description and had falsely assumed he was the one trying to kill her. And now it would look like he was kidnapping her. She had to get him to the ground before he got shot, too.

Panic pushed through her toes onto the lid of the toilet seat, sending her hurtling out the window. Preston tipped backward with her sudden weight. His arm wound around her waist, but it wasn't enough to slow her descent.

Solid dirt rushed up to meet them. Preston took the brunt of the landing, softening the jaw-jarring impact, but a nearby bush scratched against her injured arm, setting it on fire all over again. "Oh," she moaned without meaning to. She clamped her mouth shut, despite the fact she was still tumbling along the ground.

"Stop," Shaw called again into the blackness.

But the momentum of the crash kept them sliding downhill. She rolled after Preston over a rock and through the pine needles. Small plants and shrubs knocked them about like pinballs.

"Let the woman go."

Holly slowed to a halt, the bare skin below her shorts burning from the scrape of stone. A flashlight beam sliced through the dark, forcing her to lift her good arm to shield her eyes to keep from being blinded. But it didn't keep her from hearing the report of gunfire as Shaw fired what she hoped was a warning shot. But what if it wasn't?

Her heart drummed against her lungs. She couldn't handle any more gunfire. Especially not from the person supposed to be protecting her. "No. Don't."

A second shot drowned out her words.

She couldn't wait and hope Shaw realized he was after the wrong guy. She darted to her feet, reaching through the darkness for Preston. Had he been hit?

The beam of light flashed over Preston's form running toward her. He was fine. But they had to get out of flashlight range if he was going to stay that way.

His hand caught hers. Tugged her toward the trees. Toward the road. Where would they go?

Third shot. Leaves rained down from overhead. That one came a little too close to be a warning shot.

She couldn't move fast enough. Her feet seemed to trip over every pebble, her ankles twisted on uneven ground. Yet the wind brushed against her as if she were riding the Jet Ski. Her pulse certainly roared louder than an engine.

She held her injured arm up as high as she could to protect herself from running into something or falling on her face, though a stabbing pain reminded her how weak her shoulder muscle was. She probably wouldn't be able to catch herself if she tried. *Please, God, get us out of here.*

They were almost back to his truck. But that didn't change the fact a police officer was chasing them. As if running from the bad guy wasn't terrifying enough.

Shaw must have thought he *was* the bad guy. And it

didn't help that they couldn't stop sliding down the hill when the officer yelled for him to stop. He would have gladly turned himself in rather than dodge bullets.

He couldn't blame Holly for freaking out at the sight of a gun after what she'd already been through. He'd just blame her for trying to climb out the window in the first place. This was exactly why he'd needed to say goodbye. Now the people who were supposed to be helping her were hunting her.

Holly panted next to him as they burst from the woods onto the road. He pulled her arm to guide her toward the Chevy with one hand and dug in his pocket for keys with the other.

Grass crunched and footsteps pounded behind them. Static crackled. "Code eight. Requesting backup. Kidnapping in progress at Cedar Glen." The voice wheezed between sentences and grew faint.

They were going to make it. Preston would have to drive into the mountains and lie low for the night—after he got Holly to the police station. She could report him if she wanted to. At least he'd know she was safe.

Preston swung Holly toward the passenger door and let go of her hand so he could run around to the driver's side. She stared back into the woods as he turned the key in the lock and reached across to unlock her side. "Come on."

She jerked the door open with a squeak and buckled herself onto the bench seat before twisting around to watch for Shaw behind them. "He called for help. The police are going to chase us. They are going to catch you before we find your saboteur. I'm so sorry."

He started the engine and stepped on the gas, keeping his headlights off to avoid detection. Just up around the corner, he'd take a left onto the highway, then another left onto a back road. No flashing lights or sirens yet.

"They aren't going to catch us, Holly. But you are going to turn yourself in. You've got enough to worry about without running from cops and trying to solve my problem."

She covered her face. "I know. I just don't want to think about my problems anymore. It makes me feel so alone."

If only he could be there for her the way he wanted to. Preston glanced in the rearview mirror to make sure they still weren't being followed. All clear. "I know, doll." Doll. He didn't mean to keep using the old nickname. He'd practically forgotten about it until it had slipped out. He *should* have forgotten about it, given it up. Just like his sister had given up playing with her dolls.

He needed to keep his eyes on reality and not on what he wished it to be. He focused forward.

A Jeep darted onto the road in front of them. Preston slammed on the brakes to keep from rear-ending it. Holly's head whipped forward. His mouth went dry and his heart lodged itself in his throat at the idea of causing her even more pain.

The driver must not have seen him with his headlights off. Totally Preston's fault. He waved an apology, though the other guy wouldn't be able to see it.

Nope. The driver laid on the horn. Not the nicest guy in the world. Good thing they'd be turning left and would get away from the Jeep...The Jeep? The dark-colored Jeep Cherokee? The license plate number starting with 5AO.

Preston sat up straighter. Could it be? The vehicle *had* turned out of the parking lot next to Cedar Glen.

Police lights flashed in the distance coming from town. Preston had to get off the road before he was spotted. Should he take a left turn and hide out in the mountains, or should he follow the Jeep, knowing if police caught him, he'd be able to point his finger at another suspect?

The Jeep flashed a blinker to turn right into the marina. Was Preston crazy, or was God answering a prayer in that mysterious way of His? Only one way to find out. Preston swung the steering wheel right into the parking lot and parked between two larger trucks in hopes that the Chevy LUV would remain out of sight from both the driver of the Jeep and police.

"Are we getting on your Jet Ski?" asked Holly.

No lights on his Jet Ski. Wouldn't be safe to ride at night.

Speaking of lights, cop cars rocketed past, blue and red flashers spinning wildly. He and Holly were safe for the moment. Safe to follow the Jeep driver and find out if the man was truly the bomber/shooter.

Preston shook his head in response to her question. "No. The Jeep I followed in here looks like the vehicle that dropped the bomb off at your cabin earlier."

Holly spun around from facing the highway to follow his gaze. "Are you sure? There are lots of Jeeps in this area."

Preston pressed his lips together. "No, I'm not sure. But it came out of a parking lot close to the lodge. The driver could be your shooter, as well."

She clutched her injured arm and leaned forward for a better view. "What do we do?"

Good question. Preston watched the man open the driver's door and climb out under the streetlight. The bomber. "We follow to—"

Holly gasped. "I know him."

Holly's heartbeat tripped over the shock. "I can't believe he'd try to kill me. I must have been right."

Preston twisted to face her. "You recognize him? Who is he? What were you right about?"

Holly ducked behind the dashboard even though Lee Galloway headed the opposite direction. She needed the police now more than ever. Why had she insisted on climbing out the window to be with Preston? Her fear of being left alone had gotten her in trouble again.

Preston rubbed a hand over her back. "Holly, do we need to follow him or call the police immediately?"

His touch was probably supposed to soothe frayed nerves, but the pressure found a couple sore spots that must have been new bruises from falling out the cabin window. It put her even more on edge...if possible. She wouldn't sit up. She wouldn't risk looking out the windshield. She would wait for help to arrive.

"Call the police."

"Okay. But that means we have to go into the yacht club. I don't want to leave you here by yourself. And I don't know what to tell the emergency operator, either."

Her muscles stiffened at the idea of stepping into the open with a murderer. "I can't." But what could she do? "Drive to the police station."

Silence. Followed by a deep breath. "I would love to, Holly. But then this guy could get away. And also, the police might be so busy arresting me that they wouldn't listen to what we have to say."

She dug her fingernails into the old vinyl seat. She didn't want Preston to get arrested.

"Doll, why are you so scared?"

Doll. She'd loved the name when they were dating, but now the man wanted nothing to do with her. She was more of a dilemma than a doll.

What if Preston took off after the bomber was arrested, but the man got out on bail a second time and tried to kill her again? She'd have nobody to look out for her then. No fiancé. No childhood sweetheart. Nobody. Would she ever learn to look out for herself? She had to.

"That's Lee Galloway." She peeked to make sure the coast was clear before sitting up. "Caleb is defending him on murder charges even though Lee overheard me advising Caleb not to. Lee's rich wife caught him cheating, which, according to his prenuptial agreement, would have kept him from getting any of her money in a divorce. But before she could file for a separation, she was found floating in the bay. He inherited everything. I…uh… I pretty much accused him of drowning her."

She'd apparently been right. No wonder Caleb wanted to defend Lee. He could relate to the unfaithfulness. How had she been able to see the truth so clearly in another man, just not the man she'd been planning to marry?

Preston stared. "You didn't think to mention this when I asked if you had any enemies?"

Holly shrugged. She hadn't imagined her opinion on the case would be worth killing over. She wasn't the prosecuting attorney. Though now she wanted to be. "I don't know why he would try to kill me. Unless…" Did he know she'd caught Caleb cheating?

"Unless…?" Preston prompted.

Did anything else make sense? "Unless Caleb dropped him as a client because he's trying to win me back."

Preston stiffened. "He is?"

Holly paused. She was talking about the man trying to kill her, and Preston wanted to talk about the man trying to romance her? "Caleb said he came up to Tahoe in hopes of getting back together." So beside the point. "Anyway—"

"He did?"

Holly closed her eyes and shook her head. What did it matter if Caleb wanted to date her if she didn't survive to go on another date? "Preston."

"Sorry." He ran fingers through his hair. "So you think Caleb might have dropped Lee's case to win you over? And now Lee sees you as a threat?"

Mentally, Holly went back over the words, over the logic. If the man killed people who got in his way, and he considered her in his way, then yes. It fit. "The person on the phone could have been Lee's new girlfriend. She definitely wouldn't want him to lose all his money." Holly gripped the old metal handle to the truck. Talking had helped ease her nerves, but as she thought about making a mad dash to the yacht club, the trembling returned.

"All right," Preston encouraged her as he gripped his door handle. "We can do this."

Please help us do this, Lord. If Lee spotted her, would he follow and try to kill her in a public place? Caleb definitely wouldn't defend him of that crime.

She yanked the handle and shoved the squeaky door open before slipping to the ground in the cool night air. Her heart shot terror through her soul with every pulse. She'd never dealt with such a cold-blooded criminal before. She liked to defend clients who appeared innocent. How had she gotten into this mess?

Preston joined her, shielding her body with his own. An owl hooted. She jumped.

She steadied herself and exhaled. One step at a time. Maybe she should move faster. She gripped Preston's hand and picked up her pace. The slap of waves against the shore and creak of boats rocking against the dock had never sounded creepier.

She froze. Boats. This was the marina where Caleb docked his cabin cruiser. What was Lee doing here?

Preston jerked to a stop, anchored in place by her hold on him. "What?" he whispered. "You don't have to worry that Lee went into the yacht club. He headed toward the dock."

That was worse. What if Lee wasn't after only her? What if he was here to hurt Caleb, as well? She might not like her former fiancé, but she didn't want him dead. "We have to save Caleb."

Preston lifted both eyebrows. "What do you mean?"

She crouched down and zigzagged from one car to the next to get closer to the water, knowing Preston would follow. But was she crazy? A moment ago, she couldn't get away from the shooter fast enough, and now she was headed straight toward him. What did she think she could do against a man with a gun? Maybe nothing. Maybe all she had to do was warn Caleb.

"The dock is one big giant square, except it's not connected on this end so boats can get into the middle. Lee will have to walk all the way around to get to Caleb's cruiser. I can swim there faster from here."

Preston jogged after her. "You can't swim. You're injured."

"I have to. I have to warn Caleb that Lee is after him."

"You don't know that."

She kicked off her sandals in the soft sand. "Why else would Lee be going out to Caleb's boat at night?"

He grabbed her good arm. "Did you consider the possibility that Caleb is part of this?"

Holly spun around to face Preston, ripping her arm from his grasp. What was he talking about? "The police already checked Caleb's alibi. Caleb may not have loved me, but he wouldn't kill me."

"You didn't think he would cheat on you, either."

Holly's mouth dropped open. How dare Preston go there? He was supposed to be helping her, and here he was, bringing up hurtful memories to hold her back.

"Yes, Caleb did cheat on me, but if Lee's trying to kill him for righting his mistake, then I can't just stand here and let it happen." She pivoted on the ball of her foot and waded out into the frigid water. Goose bumps climbed up her legs, along her spine. She shivered but pushed on. "If you really think Caleb is guilty, then you might as well go call the police. I'm swimming out to Caleb's boat."

"Wait."

She held up a hand to hush Preston. Sound carried way too well over water.

How much time did she have? Her quarrel could have given Lee the head start he needed. But she only had a short distance to go. It was nothing compared to the pool races she'd won in college. She lined her hands up in front of her body and dived under the surface. The icy water stole her breath. Her left shoulder screamed, reminding her she hadn't been recovering from a bullet wound when swimming in college.

She couldn't let it stop her. What was a little shoulder injury compared to Caleb's life? Oh, except it wasn't a little pain. The ache clawed its way up into her teeth, her temples. She moaned. Air bubbles floated toward the surface.

Three more strokes, then she'd take a breath. One, ouch, three. How did the night seem so calm when her insides rocked turbulently?

She had to be splashing up a storm. Would Lee overhear? Shoot her from the dock? Would she and Caleb both die because she thought she'd been stronger than she really was? *The Lord is my strength.*

One stroke at a time. Right arm. Left ar—

Right arm only. She folded her left arm to her chest and kicked harder.

Maybe Preston had been right. Maybe she shouldn't have tried to swim with an injury. She gasped for a breath, but with one arm clenched to her chest, she couldn't fully rotate her face to the sky. Water filled her mouth.

A strong arm wrapped around her waist and pulled her up to inhale. Preston. Her eyes flew up to meet his as he flipped her onto her back and pulled her along. She never would have made it on her own. How was she going to survive after he went back into hiding? She gulped oxygen and pushed the fear out of her mind as he towed her toward the ladder at the stern of *Knot Guilty*.

"Thank you for coming," she whispered. He probably shouldn't have. She'd been thinking of Caleb's safety, but what about Preston's? Nobody was supposed to see him.

Preston eased her next to the ladder and let her go. "I'm not going to risk my identity being revealed to save you from a bomb, then let you swim alone out to where the bomber is headed."

She still wanted to be mad about his insensitivity earlier. But he was there for her when she needed him even if it got him in trouble. "I'm sorry."

"Doesn't matter anymore. Now climb up there and get Caleb off the boat before Lee reaches us."

Footsteps on the dock echoed in the night. The sound of her heartbeat threatened to drown it out. She gripped the ladder with her right hand and tucked her knees into her chest to place her feet on the bottom rung. Water ran down her skin as she hoisted herself into the cool air. She ignored the stinging breeze and padded through the puddles her arrival created on the rubber decking.

"Caleb," she whispered. What if she had to go down into the cabin to find him and then Lee caught them both there? Was Preston watching? Would he be able to help in time?

She rounded the corner slowly. Caleb sat with feet propped on the bow, looking up at the stars. She wouldn't have to go down into the cabin after all. Her heartbeat slowed. God was going to get her through this. She took a step forward.

The cabin hatch popped open, separating her from Caleb. Long, dark hair appeared first. Then slender arms and a trim body wearing leggings and flip-flops. The woman had her back to Holly, but Holly would have recognized the contour anywhere. Denise Amador.

SIX

Holly covered her mouth to keep from gasping. No, Caleb wasn't cheating on her anymore, but he must have been lying when he said he'd come up to Tahoe to try to work out their relationship.

Was there really a chance he'd quit representing Lee to make her happy? He obviously didn't care that much.

"What time are you taking me to Thunderbird Lodge tomorrow, babe?" Denise asked.

Holly hadn't thought the moment could get any worse. But Thunderbird Lodge? Unbelievable. Caleb was planning to take the other woman to the very venue Holly's parents had rented for their wedding at two thousand dollars an hour. Her skin warmed despite her recent swim—a swim she'd made to save Caleb's life. He didn't deserve it.

"Ten o'clock, but you're staying on the boat, remember? I have a meeting planned."

What did he mean he had a meeting planned? He'd had a wedding planned. Until Holly canceled it.

The woman pivoted gracefully to close the hatch. Her eyes locked onto Holly. She froze. "Um… Caleb?"

Caleb looked up lazily. He focused past Denise. He jumped to his feet. "Holly? What are you doing here?"

She stared as her brain listed off winning arguments

she could use against her ex to get him a guilty verdict were she to accuse him of unfaithfulness in a court of law. But she didn't have the time for that argument here.

The man darted around Denise to plead his case. "Make no mistake, this isn't what it looks like." He gripped Holly's elbows.

She winced and pulled away. And not just because of her bullet wound.

He focused on the bandage. "What happened? Did you really swim with that injury?" He scanned the rest of the boat then looked off toward the shore. "Did the police give you a ride out here? They should be protecting you."

Holly shook her head. How she'd got there wasn't important. She glanced down the dock at a figure headed their direction. "Did you drop Lee Galloway as a client?"

Not even confusion could mar Caleb's classic good looks. "What?"

She backed up toward the ladder. Caleb might not need to be rescued after all, but *she'd* be better off if Lee didn't see her. "I think Lee's after me because I accused him of murder and told you not to represent him. He's headed out here now. I was worried you'd dropped him as a client to win me back, and he might be after you, too."

Denise guffawed. "You think Caleb is trying to win you back?"

Was that all the other woman had heard? Of course, Denise probably cared more about keeping her man than the threat on Holly's life.

The situation on board the boat clearly wasn't what Holly had expected. Maybe Preston was right about Caleb. Or maybe Denise had actually hired Lee as a hit man. And Lee was headed out to collect payment from her.

Holly stepped back. She had to get away.

"Actually." Caleb cleared his throat. "I did drop Lee."

Denise spun on him. "What?"

The nearness of Lee's footfalls didn't leave Holly time to try to figure out what was going on. Not that she'd want anything to do with the lover's spat were her life not in danger. She ducked behind the cabin to climb down the ladder. She'd warned Caleb, and now she had to worry about herself.

"Hold on, Denise." Caleb held up a finger. "Holly, wait here. I don't want you swimming alone in the dark. I'll tell Lee that I've changed my mind and that I'll take his case to get him to leave. Then we'll head down to the police station together and tell Officer Shaw what's going on."

Whether or not Holly chose to trust Caleb, she couldn't trust Denise. There was no way she was staying on board with the other woman and a killer.

The boat rocked. The click of footsteps announced Lee's arrival.

Holly caught her breath. She motioned for Caleb to go face Lee as he'd suggested. Even if the gunman was here to kill him, Caleb could smooth-talk his way out of becoming fish food. He could smooth-talk his way out of anything. Case in point, the girlfriend who was staying loyal to him despite his pathetic attempts at reuniting with Holly.

Caleb squeezed her hand before stepping sideways into Lee's line of sight. "Lee," he greeted the man with a little too much enthusiasm.

Holly swung her legs over the ladder and flinched. What if Lee's only response was that now-familiar pop of gunfire?

Caleb cleared his throat. "I didn't know you were in Tahoe, but I'm so glad to see you."

Oh boy. Laying it on a little thick, even for Caleb. How had she ever fallen for the attorney's lines?

"You are?" Lee's voice lowered in disbelief. He was going to be a tougher sell than she'd been.

Holly descended into the welcome concealment of the lake. Preston silently bobbed next to the ladder. His breath warmed her shoulder, reminding her she wouldn't have been able to do this alone. She could barely swim. And worse, Lee might still come after her if Caleb failed to pacify him or Denise gave away Holly's whereabouts.

Caleb's usual sophisticated chuckle returned. "I've been thinking about your case, Lee, and I want to represent you after all. Holly is probably going to leave the firm now that we're not getting married, so her opinion shouldn't affect my clientele."

That was a smart angle. He was even trying to get Holly off the man's hit list. Or maybe he was trying to get back into Denise's good graces. Either way, what mattered was that Caleb got Lee to leave without trying to kill anyone else.

Holly closed her eyes and awaited the man's response.

Lee cleared his throat. "That sounds fair."

Hope slowed Holly's heartbeat.

"You saved his life," Preston whispered. "Now let's get you to safety and call the police."

She wouldn't argue this time. She'd be glad to get away from her ex. Lifting her knees to her chest, she pushed off the boat's smooth surface with her feet to build as much momentum as she could for a backfloat toward shore. She wished she were strong enough to let Preston swim ahead and reach land and call the police sooner, but she wasn't. Neither physically nor emotionally.

Holly kicked her legs and waited until they were a safe distance away from the boat before sharing her thoughts aloud. "Denise was there."

Preston took a couple more strokes before responding. "I heard."

"She wasn't happy to see me."

"Well, she should have been. You might have just saved her life."

"Maybe." No gunshots had been fired yet anyway. Though the woman had looked angry enough to turn on Caleb herself.

Holly's foot hit sand. She stopped kicking to let her feet sink down to the ground. Her arm didn't hurt as much as before, but all the energy from her desperate swim had drained away, leaving her limbs sluggish and weak. She trudged up the embankment, wringing water from her shirt.

Preston grabbed her hand to speed up her movement. "No, you *did* save her. Look. Lee is on his way back."

So much for a break. Holly's adrenaline shifted into overdrive. She raced after Preston, yanking her hand away from his to scoop up her sandals. He snatched his sweatshirt and running shoes.

They ducked behind a tree as Lee rounded the corner of the dock. She leaned back to catch her breath and to balance as she slid her toes into the grooves of her sandals.

Preston laced up his sneakers, using the same tree for cover. "We can't get to the yacht club to call the police before he leaves now."

Holly turned her head to peek around the tree toward the building on the other side of the parking lot. If they stepped into the open, it would give Lee a clear shot. She leaned against the tree again, but she wouldn't give up.

"Caleb could have called the police," she suggested. She would have if she were him. *Please, Jesus. Please, Jesus.*

As if on cue, blue and red lights flashed across Preston's face. They were saved.

* * *

Preston stood and watched a single police car pull into the marina parking lot. Lee slowed his steps and scanned the area as if looking for an escape route. Would a lone cop be able to take him?

A second police car turned off the road. Maybe God was actually on Preston's side for a change this time.

Lee shoved his hand into his jacket pocket. Was he grabbing a gun?

The cop cars slowed to a stop. It took a moment for Preston to realize they were surrounding the Chevy LUV. Caleb must not have called the police after all. These were the officers tracking down Preston.

He groaned and dropped his head back.

"What?" Holly asked.

He didn't want to answer. Didn't want to burst her bubble of optimism. But she'd find out anyway. "It's Shaw. He's not after Lee. He's after me for kidnapping you."

"That doesn't have to be a bad thing," Holly reasoned. "Shaw knows what I've been dealing with. He knows the bomber drives a navy blue Jeep. If I can get to him, I can tell him who Lee is."

True. Though getting to Shaw would be a problem with Lee standing in the way.

Lee headed toward his Jeep on their side of the parking lot. Holly's fingernails dug into Preston's arms. So much for that plan.

"Hey," Shaw yelled in their direction.

Had he seen them? Or had he seen Lee?

Lee ignored the officer and kept walking toward his vehicle.

Shaw intercepted. Had he realized Lee was headed toward the Jeep with the license plate he'd been looking for? "Excuse me, sir, I have a couple questions for you."

Preston closed his eyes and leaned his forehead against Holly's. This was it. The man after Holly was about to be arrested, and Preston was going to have to say goodbye to her. He pulled away and looked for the whites of Holly's eyes in the darkness. If only things had gone differently for them.

"Sir, I need to ask you a couple questions." Shaw cleared his throat. "I'm looking for a man and a woman who were driving that turquoise Chevy LUV over there."

Holly's eyes widened. Preston shook his head in disbelief. This wasn't what he'd meant by things going differently. Shaw was seriously using the suspected murderer as a witness in an investigation?

Preston peeked around the tree again to find Lee staring at the Chevy. The killer couldn't know it was the vehicle Holly had been in.

Officer Shaw pulled out his phone and flipped through a couple screens. He turned the phone toward Lee. "Here is a picture of the woman we're searching for. The man with her is about six feet tall with dark blond hair. He was last seen wearing a camouflage sweatshirt."

Preston balled the sweatshirt in his fist.

Holly covered her face. "Please don't tell me Shaw just showed my picture to the guy trying to kill me."

Preston didn't take his eyes off Lee to answer.

The man stood up straight. Scanned the area. Looked back toward the dock.

The rumble of a boat engine pierced the silence. Preston turned to watch what Lee must have been watching— Caleb's cabin cruiser taking off into the night. There went the one guy who could have come out to talk to police and ended all this.

And Lee was smart enough to put the pieces together. He'd realize Caleb's sudden departure had been related to

Holly's presence at the marina. Which would only make sense if she'd seen Lee, realized he was after her, and warned Caleb. And in that case, Lee would also have to find Caleb and kill him immediately, or there would be another arrest warrant on his head.

Holly buried her face in Preston's chest and moaned. She would have figured it out, as well. Poor thing. She'd made the honorable choice and tried to save Caleb's life, but her actions had put the attorney in even greater danger. At least Caleb was safe for the moment.

Lee rocked back and forth. "What's the couple wanted for, Officer?" he asked.

Didn't Shaw see the man's discomfort? Of course, a cop might assume the man was scared about being in the same area as wanted criminals. "That's police business. Have you seen them or not?"

Lee shook his head. "Unfortunately not, sir."

Shaw studied him. "Thank you for your help. If you see anything suspicious, please contact the police station immediately."

Lee nodded. But instead of continuing on toward his Jeep, he turned around.

Holly craned her neck to watch with Preston. "What's he doing?"

Well, he wasn't going into the yacht club for a drink. "He knows we're here," Preston whispered.

Lee shoved his hands into his pockets and headed past the officers, toward the dock.

Holly gasped. "He's looking for us because he wants to find us before police do."

"Don't worry." It was a bold move. But one that would leave Lee in proximity to be captured by police as soon as Holly told Shaw what was really going on. Preston tilted his head toward Shaw. "You're up."

She shivered in the cool air. "I won't see you again, will I?"

Preston rubbed her clammy arms for warmth. And because he'd never get the chance again. "Only God knows."

Holly didn't move. "What are you going to do without your truck?"

He chuckled. That was the least of his worries at the moment. But it was nice to know she cared. "I'll be fine. Now you go talk to Shaw so I can be sure *you're* fine."

She nodded. "I'm still going to research the helicopter crash."

"I know." He would expect nothing less. Though she'd probably find another fiancé to distract her from thoughts of him. She was never alone long. Which shouldn't bug him so much.

"You saved my life, and I want to save yours." She rubbed a hand over his biceps, looked up into his eyes.

If ever there was a moment to kiss a woman, this was it. Except for the fact it went against everything he wanted for her. He had to let her move on.

He stepped away. Dropped his hands. "Good-bye," he said. The word sucked all the air out of his lungs, like diving into the lake had done earlier. Though this time he wouldn't be following her.

She turned. Her silhouette moved through the trees. In a moment she'd step out into the parking lot.

Preston waited. If the cops came after him, he'd run, but he wasn't going to leave until he knew Holly was safe.

Officer Shaw planted his hands on his hips and faced the second officer. "I think we're being taken for a ride."

Oh, good. The lawman was finally figuring out the Lee Galloway connection.

"I don't think Holly Fontaine is in any danger at all."

Holly's shadow froze between him and the police. Preston gritted his teeth. What was the man talking about?

"If this is a kidnapping, she was an awful willing victim."

Preston ran his hands through his hair. Granted, there had been no kidnapping. That didn't mean Holly wasn't in danger.

The second officer crossed his arms. "I was a little suspicious about how she kept a man out of the computer room at the lodge. The chair had been knocked down, and she'd passed out on the floor. If somebody really wanted to kill her, she would have been dead."

Shaw nodded. Holly's profile whipped around as if she were turning to look for Preston.

Preston gave a small shrug, though she wouldn't be able to see it. She wouldn't have a choice now but to tell the authorities about him. She'd threatened as much, and now he understood. This was the position he'd put her in. He'd figure out what he was going to do later. For now, Holly just needed to get help.

A third cop joined them. "So what about the bomb? That was a definite attempt to kill her."

"Unless…"

Unless what? Preston reached his arms out helplessly before dropping them to his sides. This was getting ridiculous.

"Unless she brought the bomb, planning to use it on her former fiancé's boat. This is supposed to be the weekend of her wedding, and the man she was engaged to marry cheated on her. It actually makes more sense she would want to take him out rather than the other way around, doesn't it?"

Preston bent over and put his hands on his knees.

"You mean, she accidentally detonated the bomb in her

own cabin, then faked the shooting to make it look like she is the victim here?"

With the backlighting of parking lot lights, Preston could make out the silhouette of Holly's hands folded in front of her face. She'd be praying for help, no doubt.

"It makes sense," reasoned Shaw.

"Then who is the owner of the Chevy LUV?"

"The bomb maker. He's got to help her out of this so he doesn't get in trouble."

Holly hadn't moved. And he didn't blame her. He knew what it was like to be presumed guilty. She just needed to get out into the open before Lee circled back through the woods from the lake and found them.

Shaw pointed down toward the dock. "And it isn't over yet, boys. You know who docks in that last, empty boat slip, don't you?"

The other two men looked at each other in question.

"Caleb Brooks," Shaw answered for them.

"You mean she's here to try to kill him again?"

Oh no.

"Oh yes." Shaw nodded. "It's the only scenario that makes sense."

Holly's figure spun and charged back in Preston's direction, away from the police in the parking lot. Her sandals slapped against her heels. Her feet crunched dry pine needles.

All three officers drew guns and turned toward the woods.

A huge smile spread across Shaw's face. "We've got her."

SEVEN

Holly held her good arm in front of her as she charged into darkness. Had Preston left already? Was she going to run into Lee?

If she turned herself in to the police without Caleb, they'd be so busy questioning her and suspecting her of attempted murder that they might not listen to her warning about the real killer. And Caleb wouldn't know Lee had found out they were onto him. She'd basically be leaving her former fiancé to a death sentence. But since she knew where Caleb was headed the next day, she could get to him and alert him in time. They could go to the police together. Then Shaw would realize she wasn't trying to kill Caleb when the man explained she'd actually saved his life.

A bright beam spotlighted a tree in front of her. *Oh no.* A flashlight. A second beam bounced through the branches. The police were going to search the woods for her.

Her heart hammered in her ears as she raced over uneven ground. The bullet wound on her arm throbbed. Were they going to shoot at her again if they found her? She hadn't done anything to merit Shaw drawing his weapon.

Police should be chasing down Lee. Though maybe

chasing her would lead them to Lee. What was God's promise about all things working together for good for those who loved Him?

A warm hand hooked her elbow, swinging her around toward a tree. Lee or Preston? Should she scream?

A salty palm clamped over her mouth. Bile rose in her throat until she sucked in a breath and recognized the woodsy scent.

The earthquake inside stilled. She wasn't captured. And even better, she wasn't alone. She sank against Preston's solid body in relief. His hands released her, though, and she had to push against his chest to steady herself. "Officer Shaw thinks I'm trying to kill Caleb."

"I heard," he whispered. The stubble on his jaw rubbed her temple as he spoke, triggering memories of long moonlit walks. He sounded just as calm and confident now as he had then. How was that possible? Maybe he had a plan.

"What do we do?"

Rays of light bounced closer. Should they run? Or climb a tree? Or hide behind a log? They had to do something.

"You could turn yourself in. At least that way you won't get shot."

But she was innocent. And she wasn't going to settle for going to prison over death. Of all people, Preston should be able to understand that. Besides… "Caleb is going to Thunderbird Lodge at ten o'clock tomorrow. If we can get there, I can warn him Lee knows I'm onto him and take him to police headquarters with me. That way, police can remove me from their suspect list and stop wasting their time shooting at us."

One beam of light arced their direction. "Did you hear that?" asked an officer.

Holly pressed her lips shut and held her breath. Unfortunately the deafening drumbeat of her pulse couldn't be quieted.

Preston crouched close to the ground. Was he ducking out of sight? Why had he left her standing alone? She sank into a squat in front of him.

His hands fumbled along the ground. Had he dropped something? She squinted, as if doing so would help her see in the dark.

Warm breath brushed over her ear, sending even more shivers down her spine. "Look out toward the lake," he whispered.

Holly turned her head and focused on the silver night beyond the trees. Movement. A figure. Lee? No, there was another figure. And another. Two of them lifted the shape of a kayak over their heads. Kayaking at night?

"Starlight tour," Preston whispered. "We're going to join them."

Holly lifted an eyebrow even though he couldn't see it. She was all for slipping quietly onto the lake, but that wouldn't happen unless they could get to the beach without being spotted.

"See anything?" The cop's voice spoke from the other side of the tree they hid behind.

Holly froze, the blood in her veins turning to ice.

"Not yet. Are you sure you heard something over there?" Shaw's unmistakable rasp.

"Yes."

The far flashlight pointed out beyond them. "Could have been that group of tourists."

Holly strained her ears to make out the faint sound of laughter in the distance.

"I don't think so."

Preston's hand rose in front of her face. It clutched something round. A rock. He cocked his arm back and released. Silence. Then a small thud came from the direction of the road.

Both flashlight beams swung away from them, toward the sound. "What was that?" asked Shaw.

Holly closed her eyes, praying the footsteps would fade away. It was their only chance.

"I heard it, too," the second officer confirmed.

"Back me up," Shaw ordered. "I'm going to investigate."

"What about—"

"Tourists."

Holly clutched Preston's hand in thanks. He'd done it. Whether he agreed with her about tracking down Caleb or not, he'd created the escape route she needed.

Police boots crunched through grass. As soon as she couldn't hear the rustling anymore, she'd know they were safe to move. Just to be sure, she'd wait another minute or so.

Preston's hand pulled. He wasn't so cautious. "Come on. We don't want to miss the kayak tour."

Holly swallowed. Heading out on the water with both police and a killer after her felt a little bit like volunteering to be a sitting duck.

He stopped tugging and knelt by her side. "They're going to call for backup, Holly. A whole search party will be combing the woods soon, not to mention Caleb's nightmare of a client trying to hunt you down. You ran back to me for help, so let me help you."

He was right. He'd taken a risk just by waiting in the woods for her. Plus, God had answered her prayer for the police to head the other direction. That had to be some kind of sign. She trembled but nodded.

"Here." He passed his dry sweatshirt to her. "I probably shouldn't be wearing this anyway now that police have it on my profile."

Holly took the cozy material without argument. Preston didn't need to know she'd slept with the last sweatshirt she'd borrowed from him for a year after his funeral. "Thank you."

"You're welcome. Now let's go."

Staying low, they made their way out to the lake. Preston held a hand in front of her to keep her in the woods as he looked up and down the beach. She scanned the area, as well. Nobody but tourists.

Preston straightened and strode out into the moonlight in the middle of the group, pulling her with him. "Hey, this looks awesome. Do you guys have a couple old kayaks we could buy from you?" He motioned to his damp apparel. "We tried going for a swim, but it's still a little too cold to be enjoyable at night."

Holly glanced behind her in case the police or Lee overheard and recognized Preston's voice. But that was silly. Nobody knew what his voice sounded like, let alone that he existed.

A little bearded man in a boonie hat and life vest stepped forward. "Usually I rent out kayaks, but as we are going to be replacing the old ones soon, I reckon I could sell them to you now if you have enough cash."

Holly glanced sideways at Preston, her fingers itching with anxiety. Would he have cash with him? She didn't.

"How much?" Preston asked.

"Two hundred apiece."

The man might as well have knocked her out with an oar and called the police to pick her up. Nobody carried that much money on them.

Preston pulled a wad of cash from his pocket. "Sold."

What? Did Preston carry hundred-dollar bills? Where did he even get income?

"You're not going to barter? Then I guess I'll throw in oars and life vests. I'm Anthony, by the way."

"Thank you, Anthony. That's a good deal."

That *was* a good deal. Since they weren't renting, they wouldn't have to sign their names on a waiver or go through the normal safety speech. She wouldn't take time to question further, just grabbed a life jacket and oar from the rack. Sliding off her sandals, she dragged the kayak Anthony pointed out into water that didn't seem any icier than her current body temperature.

Most everybody else already had their kayaks on the lake, so if the police showed up at that moment, she might blend in. She watched the woods for movement while steadying the craft to stick a leg into the opening. It rocked, but she'd find stability after climbing inside. She whipped the other leg up and grabbed the edges of the seat, pulling her abs tight over the butterflies fluttering underneath. Tumbling overboard was not a good way to make an escape. The kayak shifted back and forth slightly before finding balance.

Eager chatter surrounded her. She gave a fake laugh to fit in. Beams of light emerged from the trees. Her laugh erupted into a volcano of anxiety. Where was Preston?

"You're okay." Preston glided by. "Just follow me behind Bonsai Rock." He kept an eye on Holly as he pushed his oar against the water to slip out of sight, around the edge of the giant boulder with a small tree growing on top. She'd need to calm down before she tipped her kayak.

Her paddle slapped the water. Rowing with an injured arm couldn't be easy. If they avoided detection, would she even be able to make it to the cave? Did they have a choice? They couldn't go back to his family cabin to sleep. Or her cottage at the lodge. Or even the Chevy.

Her kayak bumped into his. He reached over to hold her in place with one hand and dug his oar into the side of the rock with the other to anchor them.

She lifted her oar to rest across the front of the kayak. Her breath puffed loudly in the quiet night. Preston didn't think anyone would be able to hear from shore, but how long would they have to stay hidden before Shaw and the other officer disappeared back into the forest?

Anthony paddled by. "Isn't it peaceful out here?"

Holly looked at Preston. The moon lit the fear in her eyes. Yeah. He didn't feel much peace, either.

A flashlight beam illuminated Anthony's back. "Sorry, folks. We'll have a better view of the night sky when we get farther away from the lights. Let's paddle out deeper."

A second beam bounced from kayak to kayak. At least Preston and Holly were hidden behind Bonsai Rock, but if they didn't keep up with the group for the beginning of the tour, then they'd be sure to stand out as soon as they tried to paddle away.

"Hey," a shout called from land.

Holly's cold hand reached for his at the sound of Shaw's voice. If the cops grabbed kayaks of their own, there was no way he and Holly could get away. Maybe this wasn't such a good idea after all.

The circles of light skimmed across the water, toward the docks. Preston shifted his craft forward to see where they were going. A man in the distance held a gun by his side. A tall, lanky man. Lee.

"Stop. Police." Had Shaw recognized Lee from the parking lot, or had the officer only seen movement and mistaken Lee for Preston?

The shadow darted into the trees. The cops raced away

in pursuit. They were finally after the right guy, whether they knew it or not. Once they caught him, they'd be able to rearrange the pieces of their puzzle into the correct order.

"Where are they going?" Holly whispered, since she couldn't see.

Preston faced her again. "They're chasing Lee."

Holly dropped backward to rest her head on the kayak, arms flung wide. She stared up at the stars. "Thank You, Jesus."

Preston smiled at her relief. The girl rode her emotions like she rode a wakeboard, whereas he snorkeled with his feelings underneath the surface. What would it be like to wakeboard again? Now wasn't the time to find out.

He gave Holly's kayak a little shove. They had a lot of paddling to do. She trailed behind him as best she could with her injury, and he slowed to give her breaks here and there.

"You're taking us to Cave Rock, aren't you?" she asked after what must have been at least an hour of exertion.

"Unless you have a better idea." Would she be upset? The hole in the seventy-five-foot stone outcropping above the highway was not the kind of accommodations lawyers were used to.

She straightened out her crooked rowing and looked up at the massive shadow ahead of them. "The middle-school me would be jealous."

Middle school. A lifetime ago. Back when he'd shared with Holly the history of the Native Americans and their link to the caves. Back when he'd first started to think about kissing her but could only work up the courage to put a frog in her shoe.

He studied her profile with the pixie haircut and pert nose. Yeah, his middle-school self would be jealous of him, as well. Strike that. His middle-school self would be jealous of the old Preston. Nobody would want the life he had now.

She looked back over her shoulder. "Have you stayed here before?"

He sliced the water to glide past her, closer to the boulders where they could park the kayaks for the night. In the morning, they'd paddle to his parents' cabin to retrieve the old Jet Ski for the trip to Thunderbird Lodge. "No. I had the cabin."

She bobbled after him. "Where are you going to stay now?"

He'd worry about that once he made sure she was taken care of. Her life mattered more than his. "I don't know."

"You don't know?" She pulled her oar against the water a couple times to catch up. "Can you even rent a place without credit? And where do you get money? You can't be legally employed without a Social Security card."

The hazards of playing dead. "I work odd mechanic repair jobs."

She snorted. "Must pay pretty good for you to carry around all that money."

He'd stuffed the wad of cash into his pocket when grabbing his belongings from his parents' cabin. "It pays okay. I don't usually spend much."

It wasn't like he had anyone to impress or enjoyed traveling by himself. All he had to do was exist. He rowed to the side of a boulder at the base of the caves to climb out onto dry land.

"Are you lonely?" Holly's question followed him.

He pushed to stand and hauled the kayak up behind him. He ignored the scraping sound of plastic on rock just as he ignored the echo of Holly's words through the emptiness of his soul.

In Holly's world, loneliness would be a sign of failure, whereas, in his world, he wouldn't be able to succeed without being alone. Solitude was essential for his survival, as well as the survival of others. Which was why he had to keep his distance.

She reached her hand up for assistance as her kayak glided parallel to the rocky shore. His heart tripped at the idea of touching her, which was silly since they'd been holding hands all day. But this was different. This wasn't a race from bombs or bullets. This was a purposeful connection.

He'd tell himself it didn't have to be different. He'd disregard the way her presence scratched his itch of longing. The fact was that the more time he spent with her, the more time he'd want. So he'd have to get away—refuse to "scratch" no matter how soothing it felt in the moment.

Her fingers slid around his palm. He bent his knees to secure himself to the ground and hoist her to her feet. Now he just needed to let go.

Her eyes caught his as she stepped to the bank with him, and he couldn't help but study her in return. The soft moonlight hid the stress from her day, softened the worry lines and gave her skin a youthful glow. Too bad he knew such a serene moment could never last. He uncurled his fingers to step away.

She gripped his hand tighter, drawing his attention back to her searching expression. "You didn't answer my question."

He'd wanted her to forget. "What?"

She stepped closer. "This afternoon, when I got to the lake, I felt more alone than I'd ever felt in my entire life. But I still have a family and friends and a reputation that makes strangers want to work with me. You have no identity. Nobody who even knows your real name. Nothing. How do you do it?"

Preston looked down at their clasped hands to avoid her probing gaze. He caught his thumb rubbing over her knuckles and registered the warmth of the caress at the same time he ended it. Being with her was so natural that he couldn't try to argue he wasn't lonely without her. He balled his fist and pulled it down to his side to keep from hanging on to her the way he wanted to. "It's not about *how* I do it, Holly. It's about *why* I do it. If the why is important enough, the how just happens."

She crossed her arms. "What does that mean? You're not answering my question."

He yanked her kayak onshore, turning from her in the maneuver. "Holly, it's not about feelings to me. Sure, I get lonely. Sure, I dream that I'm a kid again and we're doing flips off the dock and getting called up for lunch by your grandma's dinner bell, and then I wake up to realize that not only is your grandma gone, but I'm gone. I punch my pillow a few times, then go for a jog until my body hurts more than my heart so I can get on with the day."

No response.

He adjusted his shirt. Ran a hand over his head. Finally peeked over his shoulder.

She covered her mouth with a hand. Her eyebrows knit together in concern.

He rubbed at the building pressure in his temples. He didn't want sympathy. "I guess that's how I do it. But that's not what matters. What matters is protecting my family."

All right, it wasn't only his family he was protecting. If it was, he'd never have taken those pictures of Caleb and Denise together. He never would have pulled out the binoculars when he saw a car drive up to Holly's cabin.

"And protecting you."

Her hand lowered from her mouth. "Maybe you should leave that job to God," she said.

As if God was enough for her. Did she really trust God's direction, or did she just pray for protection as she went off and did her own thing? He bit his tongue. He'd try talking her language instead of making accusations. "Maybe God is using me to keep you safe."

She pressed her lips together as she studied him. "So if God would use you to keep me safe, then why wouldn't He use me to help you find out the truth about sabotage? That's kind of a double standard you've got going there."

Really? Theology at midnight? After the day they'd had, she should just be thankful to be alive. She should be thanking him. And if she was going to be mad at anybody, it should be her ex.

"You're telling me *I* have double standards? You're upset I care about keeping you safe, while at the same time, you have not only let Caleb off the hook for this whole mess, but you've asked me to help save his life."

Hand on her hip. "This has nothing to do with Caleb."

"It has everything to do with Caleb." She may be the lawyer, but he had plenty of evidence in his favor. He ticked off the list on his fingers. "Caleb was the one who took Lee Galloway as a client in the first place, despite your better judgment. And Caleb was the one who cheated, causing you to break up with him. And Caleb was the one who dumped the crazy client to try to win you back even though—and I don't know why we are so surprised by this—he's still dating someone else. Do you want me to keep going?"

She held up her hand. "No."

"Why couldn't you have said that when he proposed?"

EIGHT

Holly's fingernails dug into her palms as she balled her fists. How dare Preston disappear for four years, then come back and get mad at her for moving on without him? "You have no right."

Preston held up his hands in a shrug. "I had to come out of hiding to save you, so I think I have every right."

The nerve. "You left, Preston. You let me think you were dead. So if this is anyone's fault, it's yours."

He planted his fists on his hips. "You're right. It's too bad I'm not *really* dead. Because then you would be getting married to a player tomorrow and Lee never would have had to come after you."

She stepped back. What had Preston just said? Her mind whirled. Why would she be getting married to Caleb if Preston were dead? She'd broken off the relationship because of pictures Denise had sent her. Unless…

"What?" He shifted his weight to the other leg. His eyes flicked away warily.

She could barely breathe as she formed the words to the overwhelming idea. "Did you send me the pictures of Caleb with Denise?" *Oh no. Oh no, no, no.*

Preston opened his mouth. No words came out.

"You did!"

He reached for her. "Holly."

She stepped back and held a hand to her heart. "Were you upset because I wasn't still moping around and mourning your—" air quotes "—'death'?"

Preston's gaze bored into hers. He was as motionless as she was animated. "Of course not."

He looked so innocent that she wanted to believe ruining her relationship hadn't been his intent. But she'd also believed he was dead at one time.

"Why would you do this to me?"

"I was trying to save you."

She dropped her head back and groaned. How could the stars twinkle and shine above with such splendor and beauty when her whole world was falling apart? Because even if Preston was able to keep her alive, she was going to have to spend that life all by herself. "My hero. Able to keep me from both a relationship with you and a relationship with anyone else at the same time."

He exhaled loudly enough to draw her attention back to him. Mistake. Because he really did look like a hero in the moonlight. Damp T-shirt clinging to his muscles. No sweatshirt because he'd given it to her to wear. Determination in his eyes.

He shook his head. "Look, doll—"

Now that was too much, no matter how dashing he looked. She was not his doll. She was not his anything. Including his responsibility. She stepped forward and poked him in the chest before she could stop herself. "You don't get to call me that anymore."

"I'm sorry, Holly." He caught her hand.

She yanked it away. Because the warmth of his touch might melt her heart.

"You can think what you want, but the truth is that

when I went to sneak a peek at my nephew after he was born, I overheard my sister mention your engagement."

Aww... Her fists unclenched thinking about her new nephew. Also Preston's new nephew. Named after him, actually. Though Preston would never get to hold Pres.

"I wasn't happy at first. I mean, you were my first love. My only love."

She melted a little more. Though grudgingly. Because loving her didn't make it right for him to stalk her and snap photos of her fiancé.

"But I really did want you to be happy. So I decided to take a present over to Caleb's house and drop it off anonymously."

Really? He'd done that for her? Like the mother who gave away her baby to keep it alive back in King Solomon's day.

"And that's when I saw him with Denise."

Stupid Denise. Maybe it was all the other woman's fault. Holly needed someone to blame. Especially if she was going to let Preston off the hook. That was how her lawyer's mind worked, anyway.

"What would you have done in my shoes, Holly?"

She looked away rather than admit the real reason she was mad. She was mad he'd left her four years ago. She was mad that she'd even had to consider dating Caleb in the first place. She was mad that she liked being with Preston so much that other men didn't compare. And she was mad that he was leaving her again.

She swallowed down the squeaky voice that alerted people when she was about to cry. "Caleb was a mistake."

"You deserve better than Caleb."

She twisted her lips pensively at the thought. She didn't want to be with Caleb, but she didn't want to be single, either. "I don't do loneliness as well as you do, Preston."

He crossed his arms and stared down at the ground. Maybe he felt the same way she did. Maybe his tough-guy act was all a front. But she'd never know if he wouldn't open up and talk to her. For example, he could have told her that he was the one who sent the pictures to her when she told him about Caleb earlier that day. But no. He kept everything inside.

He wasn't the same person she used to know. He was a lone ranger.

What was worse than being alone? Feeling alone when with someone else.

Holly turned to pull her sandals out of the kayak for her hike up the hill. "I'm just going to head up to the cave. Thank you for the sweatshirt. It'll keep me warm."

Would Preston join her, or should she start getting used to his absence again? She used to imagine finding him alive. But never like this. There was usually a slow-motion run through a flowery meadow involved. Not this coldness or distance. She slipped her feet back into the leather straps and stood. Turned.

Preston's chest blocked her path. Her breath caught. Her hand flew to her heart. Was he going to open up now?

"I don't want to hurt you," he said.

He'd closed the space between them to tell her he didn't want to hurt her? If he didn't want to hurt her, then he shouldn't be reeling her in like a fish to discard her again. Her collarbones prickled at the chance that maybe he wasn't going to catch and release this time. She turned her hand around from her chest to his—to hold him back. She couldn't be caught this easily.

"It hurts to be near you and not know you anymore," she whispered.

His hand covered hers. "I'm sorry."

Was there any promise in his eyes? Any plans to make

it up to her? Any willingness to be vulnerable and get reacquainted? Was the moonlight playing tricks on her, or was the only glimmer in Preston's eye that of regret?

"I want you to know that when I left for my final tour overseas, I did love you very much."

Did? What good could "did" do them? "Did" was a deflated inner tube.

She dropped her hand. "Well. I guess that's that."

She stepped onto a rock to climb away from her childhood sweetheart. Once in the cave, she could hide her tears. Though she wouldn't blame them on Preston. She'd tell herself she was crying over the attempt on her life, and about being under suspicion by the police department, and sleeping by herself in a cave the night before she was supposed to be getting married. She'd refuse to admit that if Preston still loved her, all of those things would have been nothing compared to the reward of finding out he was still alive.

Was there a chance Preston still loved her? What if he'd been trying to open up a moment ago and only stunk it up because he was out of practice with relationships?

She stopped. Turned back. "Unless you want to take me up on my offer to help you investigate the sabotage."

He shook his head slowly. "I can't."

Figured. Though even the Lone Ranger had Tonto.

"There are some things we just can't do on our own, Preston."

He rubbed his jaw. "I'm not alone. I've got God."

So he said. But he wouldn't accept the possibility God brought him back into her life so *she* could help *him*. "Remember that scripture about how two are better than one."

"'Woe to him that is alone when he falleth; for he hath not another to help him up.'" Preston quoted from the very passage she'd been talking about, but his tone sounded darker for some reason. "I know that one well. The thing is, I was part of a team. We were supposed to be there for each other, and I let them down. Now they are all fallen. I can't let that happen to anyone else."

"I see." He'd rather suffer than feel responsible for the suffering of others. He probably told himself it was the right thing to do. He didn't realize that living in fear was as far from love as you could get. "You're afraid to love."

Though Preston watched Holly climb to the cave, her words remained. *You're afraid to love.* No. She didn't see at all. He was doing her a favor. He was putting her life above his own. He was stepping out of the picture so she could move on and be happy. Just like he'd tried to do with her and Caleb.

Yeah. That had worked out well.

He climbed up after her to sit outside the cave and keep watch. The cold stone seeped through his soggy jeans. The jagged rock dug into his spine. Hopefully, Holly was more comfortable inside, curled up with his sweatshirt. She had to be exhausted.

He might not be able to sleep, but he was used to that. Running from the enemy. Finding places to hide. Staring at the stars alone. It was no life for Holly. Why couldn't she accept the fact?

Sure, she was lonely. He got that. But that didn't mean she should help him come out of hiding. She thought she could prove him innocent. But what if she couldn't? What if she spent all her time with him and didn't get a chance to live her own life? And he could forget the idea that he might be able to keep his existence a secret. If she didn't leak it to the police, her mom would be sure to figure it out. Then he'd have to bide his time, waiting for a court date. And what if the judge ruled him guilty and he ended up in prison? How would her relationship with a convict affect her reputation? He was afraid—

Afraid. But not in the way Holly meant it. He wasn't afraid to love. He just chose not to love. It was the smart choice. The one that would keep Holly safe.

He sighed and leaned back to look at the stars. A satellite glowed as it inched across the horizon. There were more satellites now than when he used to stargaze from the dock with Holly. Meteor showers with her had been the best.

A dull ache radiated from his sternum. He shifted to shake it loose. It didn't budge. He crossed his arms to smother it. The throbbing intensified.

Why did being with Holly have to make him long for more? He'd been praying for more for years, begging God to grant him justice. But no matter what direction he took, it was always a dead end. His enemies continued to get away with murder.

And now he'd be without a place to stay. Much like David when he'd run from Saul in Bible times. They were both innocent, and both had had to take refuge in the wilderness. But God had brought David out of it.

Preston had given up hoping for a second chance when Holly got engaged. He'd finally accepted the life he would have to live. Which made this situation even crueler. Just when he'd made peace with reality, she had to reappear and tempt him to dream again.

And that dream was so enticing He'd almost given in. He'd even stepped forward with intent to dip his head to whisper a kiss across her soft lips. But if he'd have done that, he'd never have been able to let her go. The lock on the door of his heart would be busted, and the whole door would likely get knocked off its hinges as his feelings poured out. He had to be strong. He had to refuse to let her sacrifice her future for the chance at a life with him. Because that chance had passed. Hadn't it?

What if David had given up?

The question came from out of nowhere, making Preston's palms itch. He didn't want to think about how David's life had been restored. How the man had been crowned king. How God had granted him justice.

David had been anointed. God had made him promises. Preston didn't have any such divine destiny on his own life. His story was just one of the many tragedies that took place every day in the world. Who was he to ask for more?

He was no David, but what if he compared himself to the persistent widow? Jesus had told the story of a woman who continued to go to an ungodly judge for help. The judge didn't help her because it was "the right thing" to do, but so she would leave him alone. Jesus had told the parable as an example of how to pray. Preston used to pray like that. Nothing had come of it, so he'd stopped. He'd given up. He'd been afraid of getting let down again.

Afraid. There was that word again. His heart tapped against his chest as if trying to send him a message in Morse code. His lungs expanded. He blew out the deep breath.

What had the persistent widow asked of the judge? *Avenge me of mine adversary.*

Dare he make the same request? Could anything come from it or was he just setting himself up for failure again? Were those words he could whisper under his breath, and then, if it didn't work out, he could blame God? Or were they a prayer he would have to commit to with every fiber of his being? Was he willing to fall down on his face before the Lord and plead the way David had? Could he be that helpless? That relentless?

Such openness would require Preston to unlock his

feelings. David certainly hadn't kept any of his emotions bottled up inside. Was Preston ready for that?

Preston shook his head. He'd take baby steps. He'd ask for God's help, but he wouldn't accept Holly was the answer to prayer. He still had to keep Holly out of his mess for her own good. If God somehow did bring his enemies to justice and restore Preston's life, then he could open up to Holly.

"Avenge me of mine adversaries."

A little hope bubbled within. Not enough for him to sneak back into his parents' cabin to pick up the engagement ring he'd bought for Holly before he left for the Middle East, but enough for him to be able to relax back into the rock wall and breathe easier. And apparently enough for him to fall asleep.

He opened his eyes to the sun peeking over the mountains and the pink sky reflecting on the still lake. He rolled his head from shoulder to shoulder to loosen up his stiff neck, then reached both hands overhead to stretch his tight back. It would have been a gorgeous, peaceful morning if not for the murderer who might still be on the loose.

After peering into the cave to find Holly with her hands tucked under her face like a pillow, Preston headed down to the water to catch a couple fish with a stick whittled into a spear. He then struck his pocketknife against a rock and caught the sparks on a piece of tinder fungus. By the time Holly joined him, he had two trout roasting over the flames.

"Good morning." Was she still mad at him or had she gotten over whatever had caused her to explode the night before? Probably just the trauma from the day. If yelling at him had helped her cope, he would let her yell at him anytime.

She walked stiffly toward the log where he sat and gingerly lowered herself next to him. She rubbed her hands, then held her palms to the flames. "You didn't have time to make any acorn coffee, did you?"

Safe topic. Silly question. He'd consider it a truce.

"I did make some coffee, actually. But you slept so long the squirrels drank it all." Shelling and roasting the nuts had been a full day's project with his dad once upon a time. The warm, caramel-tasting beverage sure would have been more welcome than the fishy smell that made Preston's empty stomach churn.

She smiled at the fire. "Selfish squirrels."

"Here." He scooped a portion of flaky fish onto a large leaf for her. "They left you some of this."

She pinched a portion and lifted it to her tongue. "I don't think I've had trout from a campfire since the last time we went fishing together."

He studied Holly, the past blending with the present. He'd never loved fishing as much as he'd loved the quiet time with her. And she'd never loved eating fish at all. "Sorry it's not eggs Benedict."

Her eyes met his. "I'm not complaining."

His pulse skipped a beat. Should he tell her that she'd inspired him to pray the night before? That she was right about him being afraid? And that she made him want to love again? "Holly—"

She gripped his arm and pointed past him. "There goes Caleb's boat."

NINE

Holly directed Preston to pull the Jet Ski behind the boat-house to the left of Thunderbird Lodge. "We'll be out of sight over here."

It had taken longer than she'd hoped to row their kayaks to retrieve the Jet Ski and ride across the lake. Hopefully, Caleb was still there. Then she'd call the police so Caleb could vouch for her innocence, and Preston could disappear once again.

Preston parked, and she led him along the rock wall above the beach and around the side of the stone mansion toward the gazebo. She sighed as she stared at the spot where her wedding ceremony would have been held this very hour if Preston hadn't caught Caleb with Denise. Regret mixed with relief, but the truth was that she loved the idea of getting married in such a beautiful place over the idea of marrying Caleb. And Caleb was even more of a dirtbag than she'd thought, using the venue her parents had rented for their canceled wedding so he could hold work meetings and impress clients.

Preston looked around. "I always wanted to come here as a kid because I heard all about the eccentric owner, but I don't think it was available for rental or tours until recently."

"Nope." She tried to see the massive boulders and towering trees through his eyes. They definitely made the rugged point on the lake even more majestic. She and Preston had been pretty blessed to have cabins passed down to their families so they could grow up spending summers in an area that usually only the most wealthy could afford. Not to mention it was a great place for Preston to play dead. Would he return to hiding out in his cabin once Lee was caught?

They rounded the edge of the lodge. Caleb's sleek cabin cruiser rocked next to the dock. Holly's heart lurched.

Preston grabbed her hand and pulled her forward to duck behind a tree. He must have spotted the boat, too. He crouched and moved behind the hedges, toward the gazebo perched directly up a pathway from the dock.

"I can't get down there without being seen," he whispered. "Just tell Caleb what happened last night and explain how you need him to let Officer Shaw know you're not trying to kill him. Then have the police come out here. I don't want you leaving on that boat with him. I still don't trust him."

"Or Denise," she added. Couldn't leave the other woman out.

"Or Denise," Preston agreed. Probably to keep the peace.

If everything went smoothly, this thing would almost be over. The police would arrest Lee and his mistress. Holly would be safe again. Preston could go back into hiding. Hooray.

"Okay." Preston squeezed her hand. "I'll be right here if you need anything."

Holly squeezed back. He'd be right there for her until Lee went to prison. Then he'd disappear again. She smiled sadly at the man who'd once been her best friend. "I know."

She took a deep breath and slid her fingers away. She'd moved on without him before. She could do it again.

Ha. Caleb's boat mocked her as she made her way down the hill and onto the wooden planks. It represented her poor attempt at moving on without Preston.

The door to the cabin opened. Denise climbed out in a white bikini and spread her beach towel on a bench seat. She slid sunglasses on her nose before rubbing shiny oil over her legs.

Holly's stomach twisted. She'd so much rather talk to Caleb than his stunning girlfriend.

Denise tossed her hair. She did a double take when she spotted Holly on the dock.

Holly peeked up toward where Preston hid. Knowing he was on her side gave her confidence.

"You still love him, don't you?" Denise accused.

Holly's heart thumped louder. How did the woman know about Preston? And why would she think Holly still loved—

"I know it's your wedding day and all, but Caleb is with me now."

Oh. Denise thought she still loved Caleb. Holly blew air into her cheeks. "I don't want Caleb back. I'm here to tell him Lee Galloway knows we're onto him. Both you guys are in danger. You need to get to police as soon as possible."

Denise lowered her glasses to look at Holly over the rims. Her voice lowered, as well. "You're here to save our lives?"

Holly blinked. She wasn't going to get anywhere with this woman. "May I talk to Caleb, please?"

Denise pushed her glasses back up and lay down. "He's not here. He went up to the lodge to meet someone."

He'd already gone up? Holly had to warn Preston. Her

gaze flew to the gazebo. No Preston in sight, but Caleb was strolling across the grounds with another man. Hopefully, Preston had seen them coming and ducked for cover.

"And in case you have any ideas of stealing him back, honey, you should know I wasn't ever the other woman. You were."

Tingles shot through Holly's fingers and toes. She took a step back. What was Denise talking about? That didn't make any sense. When Caleb asked her out for the first time, he said he'd recently gotten out of a bad relationship. Holly had consoled him.

"No, I—"

"We never broke up. I let him date you to secure our future together."

Denise had to be lying. Holly put on her trial face. "You were going to let him marry me to secure your future?"

The woman rolled up to a seated position and propped herself up with her hands. "He wasn't actually going to marry you. He needed to find someone close to you as part of one of his cases. He said if he proposed, this other person would come out of hiding and get arrested for what he'd done."

Holly clutched her chest. Waves of anger washed over her. Caleb was after Preston. He'd been the JAG lawyer for SOAR at the time of the helicopter crash, so maybe he was privy to some information that indicated Preston was still alive. And he falsely assumed Preston had been responsible for the sabotage. Winning a case like that would elevate him to instant fame.

Was that what Denise meant by securing their future? It was all so messed up. But that wasn't the worst part. The worst part was that Caleb had manipulated Holly into believing he loved her to get to the man who really *had* loved her. And he'd let her parents spend thousands of dollars on his charade.

Her worlds spun together at a dizzying pace. Preston's innocence. Caleb's suspicion. Being stuck in the middle could crush her like ice in a blender. She gripped the edge of the boat to keep balanced.

Why hadn't anyone told her the truth to begin with? She was done with the lies. If Caleb knew Preston was alive, then there was no reason for her childhood friend to hide anymore. She'd get the attorney to believe Preston's side so he could help investigate the helicopter crash. Even if he didn't want to, he owed her big-time.

She straightened and looked up at the soaring roofs of Thunderbird Lodge towering over the rock walls. Her parents had paid good money for this place, and she was going to get her money's worth. She spun away from Denise and marched toward the stairs that would take her straight to Caleb.

Preston crouched behind the gazebo wall the moment he'd heard voices. Had Caleb already come up to the mansion for his meeting?

The voices grew louder. "So glad you decided to bring your family out to Tahoe for a vacation even though my wedding was canceled, Robert."

Preston rolled his eyes. Caleb sure seemed to be making the most of his canceled wedding. Would probably even take his girlfriend on the honeymoon he'd planned with Holly. Why was he risking his neck to save this guy's life again?

"Did the rental I recommended at the entrance to Tahoe Keys work out for you?" Holly's former fiancé schmoozed.

"Yes. Huge place on the end of White Sands Drive. Perfect. The family loves it, but, Caleb, you know I'm here on business, as well."

Preston frowned at the familiar voice. Deep. Crisp. Authoritative.

Caleb clapped his hands. "I know, and I'm pleased to report that very soon I will have finished tying up all the loose ends from Operation Desert Hope."

Preston's spine snapped straight. Heat shot from his heart and radiated out to all his limbs. His brain went fuzzy for a moment, as if he were trying to look through an unfocused lens of a camera. The lens focused. Zoomed in.

Had Caleb been investigating the failed op this whole time? He *had* been the judge advocate general assigned to the case. Maybe he'd figured out who had really sabotaged the choppers. Preston could hug him. Holly's cheating ex-boyfriend could be the answer to his prayers.

The other man cleared his throat. Where had Preston heard that sound before?

Caleb called the man Robert. It couldn't be Robert Long, could it? Preston had to peek around the wall to be sure.

Silver hair. Tall. More of a belly than Preston remembered, but if the commander wasn't active military anymore…

Preston couldn't see the man's face from behind, but he would recognize the age spots on those hands anywhere. Commander Long had been in charge of the failed op. He'd believed Preston was innocent.

"No," Long argued. "I'm here to tell you the case is closed. We're better off leaving it alone."

Preston dropped back to his hiding place. Why wouldn't Commander Long want to reveal the truth?

"Make no mistake, sir, it would help remove the tarnish from your otherwise platinum career."

Since when did Caleb care about anybody else? Wanting to reopen the case had to be a purely selfish move. It would bring the attorney fame and glory. He wasn't really concerned about Long's career.

Long was the one who cared for other people, which was why the man's response was so confusing. "I've moved on. I'm retired. This is over. And that's an order."

Was Long hiding something, or did he just want to move on with his life? The way Preston couldn't.

"Yes, sir."

"I'm leaving." The commander sounded wearier than his age would suggest. "My family is waiting for me to take them to Eagle Falls. I'm going to go enjoy the rest of my vacation, and I suggest you do the same." Long's footsteps clicked away.

Eagle Falls? Preston could meet him there. The man didn't know Preston was still alive. If he did, he might change his mind about the whole case. He might be able to help Preston fill in the missing holes in the circumstances surrounding the sabotage.

Preston had never considered meeting with the commander before because of the danger, but surely whoever killed Sergeant Beatty hadn't followed the commander on vacation.

"Caleb Brooks, I have to talk to you." An angry female voice interrupted Preston's thoughts.

Preston twisted to face the stairs, where Holly was storming up. What was she so upset about? As far as he knew, she'd come here for Caleb's help.

He leaned around the edge of the gazebo enough so Holly could see him. He willed her to look his way. She didn't. Her eyes zeroed in on the other man like lasers.

If she wasn't so angry, Preston would have left her to wait with Caleb for the police so he could go track down Commander Long. But he needed to know what was going on first.

"I can't believe you." She huffed at the top of the steps. "How dare you use me as a pawn?"

She was a pawn? For what?

Preston ducked behind the gazebo wall. Where had Holly gotten her information? And was she right?

"Holly?" Caleb's voice rose. "What are you doing here?"

"I can do whatever I want here. My parents rented this place for the day." She paused. "Do you have any idea how much they spent? Were you planning to bring your girlfriend here all along?"

Oh... Holly had talked to the girlfriend on the boat. Must not have been a pleasant experience.

"Of course not." Caleb played innocent so well.

"Denise told me *I'm* the other woman."

She was? How did that work?

"Look, Denise believes what she wants to believe."

Preston shook his head at the man's excuses. He obviously said whatever he thought would get him what he wanted in the moment. The problem was that he was so smooth it usually worked. If Caleb hadn't just mentioned Operation Desert Hope, Preston would never want to see him again.

Caleb continued, "The truth is, I dumped her right before I asked you out. But she would never leave me alone."

Would the attorney just move past his relationship lies so they could talk about the important stuff? Like getting to the police before Lee found them? Then Preston would be free to track down Commander Long.

"If you want to talk about the truth," Holly challenged,

"let's talk about who really sent me the pictures of you and Denise together."

Oh boy. Adrenaline shot through Preston's veins. He pressed into the rough rock wall to control his energy. And to move closer to Caleb to better hear the man's response.

Was this what Holly meant about using her as a pawn? Did Caleb know Preston was alive, and he'd proposed to Holly to get Preston to come out from hiding? Was this what Caleb was talking about when he told Commander Long he was about to wrap up the sabotage case? Maybe Preston should have gone to Caleb in the first place.

Caleb's tone changed—moving from defense to offense. "Who do *you* think sent them?"

"I know who sent them."

"Who?"

Preston shook his head. Would somebody just spit out his name already? This game was getting them nowhere.

"It was somebody you wanted to come out from hiding," Holly hedged. Probably second-guessing herself and afraid of the consequences should she reveal Preston's secret.

Caleb spoke just as cautiously. "Who is hiding?"

Enough. Preston stood. "I was hiding."

Caleb's eyebrows rose, though he didn't look too surprised. "Preston Tyler."

The man obviously had known Preston was alive. He must have figured Preston would want to keep Holly for himself and thus reveal his existence should someone else propose. The attorney's narcissistic brain would never have guessed Preston might let her go in order for her to be happy. But Caleb's mistake of getting caught with Denise had given him what he'd been after from the beginning. And now maybe they could both get what they wanted since Caleb had some kind of information on the sabotaged op. It was worth the risk of revealing himself. Maybe this was God's answer to his prayer for vengeance.

Holly gasped. "Preston."

"Hi, Holly." Why did she look so worried? She'd been the one wanting him to come out in the first place.

"You should have stayed hidden. Caleb thinks you're the saboteur, and he wants to take you to trial and get acclaim by smearing your name in the mud."

Oh. Good reason to look worried. Unfortunately she hadn't said as much earlier. Because it was too late now.

He ran a hand over his head. So that was why Commander Long wanted Caleb to drop the case. He didn't think Preston was responsible for sabotage. Maybe it wasn't Caleb who had info that could free him. Maybe Long was the one in the know.

"You really think I sabotaged Operation Desert Hope?" Did Caleb even care? Or was Preston just part of the man's get-rich-quick scheme?

Caleb held out his hands. "Hey, I didn't want to believe it. But Sergeant Beatty whispered to me that you were still alive, and then we found him hanged in his barracks the next morning. That was too much of a coincidence for it to be suicide. And you *were* the only soldier not in the plane crash."

Preston balled his fists. He needed to punch something. This whole time, Caleb had suspected him for the same reason he'd suspected someone else. Though Caleb didn't know the full story. "I saw a guy tampering with the helicopter right before we were to take off. I scared him away and went to tell Beatty to stop the operation, but I was too late."

Caleb eyed him. "If you're innocent, why'd you go into hiding?"

Was Caleb accusing him, or did he really want to know?

Did it matter? Preston had revealed himself, and he'd have a lot of explaining to do, whether to Caleb or someone else. "I went into hiding *because* Beatty was killed. I was afraid if I spoke to anyone else, they'd get killed, too. I decided to figure this out on my own before coming forward."

Caleb studied him. "Did you?"

Preston's heart sank. He glanced over at Holly. Looked like he might need a defense attorney after all.

She stepped forward. "Not yet, but I believe he's innocent, Caleb. And I think I saw something in the newspaper that might prove it. I just haven't been able to put my finger on it yet."

"If you say so." Caleb looked back and forth between the two of them. "You're going to turn yourself in?"

Preston reached for Holly's hand. He hated having to rely on someone else, but he'd need her now more than ever. "Yes."

Holly looked up. "At least now we can explain everything to police."

Caleb tilted his head. "What do you mean?"

Preston took a deep breath. Caleb could at least defend him in this situation if not the SOAR disaster. "The police saw my truck at the marina last night. They assumed Holly must have been trying to kill you. It's a long story, but now you can tell them she was actually trying to save you."

"You're kidding."

Preston wished he was. Their situation might be laughable if it wasn't so tragic. "Ironically, we came here trying to save you again, since Lee Galloway knows we alerted you about his intent to kill Holly."

"Oh no." Caleb blinked and looked around.

Preston followed his gaze and scanned the area. Birds twittered. A gentle breeze blew. Not a blade of grass was out of place. Would have been the perfect day for a wedding.

He glanced down at Holly. She was soon going to be out of danger from Lee and from the police. But she'd have her work cut out for her with his case.

Her wide gray eyes connected with his. She was a strong woman. Stronger than she realized. Maybe someday they'd get that second chance at the romance he used to hope for.

"I can give you two a moment alone if you want." Caleb chuckled.

The man must never have really cared about Holly at all. He was an idiot. Preston glared.

Caleb's smile faltered as he stepped back. "I should probably go call the police anyway. I didn't last night because I saw their lights in the marina parking lot and figured they had everything taken care of. I can't believe they let Galloway escape."

Preston squared his jaw. He couldn't even respond to Caleb's incompetence. One simple phone call from the attorney would have kept him and Holly from evading police and sleeping in a cave the night before. Not to mention how Caleb's trap to catch Preston had put Holly in Lee's crosshairs in the first place. Yeah, Preston had nothing to worry about if this was the guy who'd be prosecuting him in court.

Holly read his expression. "Go ahead, Caleb. We'll wait here."

Caleb walked backward down a couple of stone stairs. "You sure? Because I'm having trouble trusting Preston right now."

Preston cocked his head. Caleb had no room to talk. If anybody was untrustworthy…

Holly rubbed her free hand down Preston's arm to calm him. "Then trust me. I'm not letting him get away this time."

Caleb shook his head but continued down the stairs to his boat.

Preston exhaled to deflate his ego. No reason for the cops to get a first impression of him punching the guy in the gut—whether the jerk deserved it or not. He turned his focus to Holly. She looked especially pretty the way joy shimmered in her eyes. It made him want to hope again.

"I'm so glad you're doing this," she whispered. "You won't regret it."

He wanted to believe her. It was certainly true of the moment. No regrets. Only possibilities. Like the one of dipping his lips to hers. When was the last time he'd considered kissing her an actual possibility?

His belly warmed. His heartbeat shimmied. He looked up from her lips to read her eyes and make sure she was feeling the same way. Of course, if he was going to be her client, maybe he should wait to kiss her until after he was a free man. But her eyes held the same expectation he felt, drawing him toward her like a river's current. She was only a breath away.

His heart hammered, jarring his whole body. Or was that the hammer of a gun?

Dirt sprayed up from his feet. A slug.

What? Had the police gotten there that fast? Had Caleb told them something that would make them think Preston was armed and dangerous?

Holly jumped and clutched his arms. Over her shoulder, Preston spotted a tall, lanky man aiming a gun at them from the direction of the parking lot.

Lee Galloway had found them.

TEN

"Run." Preston pushed Holly to get her going.

She gripped her fingers and took off, hurdling stones and shrubs. Bullets pinged off boulders surrounding them. They had to sprint past the lodge to get down to the Jet Ski. That meant no cover from Lee's line of fire.

The glass from the sconce mounted on the lodge next to them shattered. Holly screamed. Should they jump off the rock wall toward the beach below, hoping the sand would be soft enough to break their fall? They could try to join Caleb in his boat and make their escape with him. Preston faced the rock wall as if he'd had the same thought.

The boat engine revved and pulled away from the dock. Holly should have known Caleb the coward wasn't going to wait around to risk getting hit by a bullet.

She yanked Preston's arm the opposite direction, pulling him to the door of the lodge. She had a better idea than relying on a liar and cheat.

"Holly, we have to—"

A bullet buried itself in the arched black doorframe. Her trembling fingers slipped from the iron handle. She gripped it a second time. Preston pushed, as well. The door swung open to usher them into the wood-paneled room with steep ceilings and a rustic chandelier. He slammed the door shut and fumbled for a lock, but it needed a key.

She hoped her plan would work. "This way."

Together, they raced down a hallway. She pounded down the spiral stairway first, missing a couple steps as gravity sped her escape.

"Holly, no. We'll get trapped in the basement."

The front door slammed open, announcing their pursuer. Holly didn't have time to explain. She motioned for him to follow her. Would his hesitance allow Lee to catch them?

Preston tensed, but jumped up onto the railing and slid silently down the staircase after her. Her pounding heart paused to offer a prayer of thanks.

"Come on," she whispered before leading him through the kitchen and down a hallway, past the maid's quarters and into a laundry room. This was the direction the tour guide had taken her, wasn't it?

Preston looked around, then focused on her, his eyes bulging. She knew what he was thinking. *Dead end.*

With her heart in her throat, she pulled open what appeared to be the door of a linen closet. The muscles on Preston's face softened as he looked past her, into a secret tunnel lined with stone.

"You're incredible." He motioned for her to enter first, then pulled the door closed behind them.

She'd almost canceled her lodge tour when Caleb hadn't been able to join her in picking a wedding venue, but Alexandria had stepped in and they'd made it a girls' getaway. Now it was just a getaway. The tunnel that used to lead the eccentric owner's exotic pets safely to the boathouse on summer visits would now lead her and Preston directly to the Jet Ski. Then they'd head straight for the police.

* * *

Preston climbed onto the Jet Ski and gunned the engine. Holly gripped his sides as he took off past Thunderbird Lodge. Lee hadn't yet emerged from the building yet, so it wasn't likely he would be able to give chase. Preston exhaled in relief.

Holly leaned toward his ear. "The police station is the other way."

Yes. Yes, it was. "We're going to Eagle Falls." He hadn't yet told her about Robert Long. "My old commander was at the lodge with Caleb. He told Caleb to drop the case, and I didn't understand why at first. But now I realize it's because Caleb thinks I'm guilty. So Commander Long must know something. I want to talk to him before I turn myself in."

Her fingernails dug into his sides. "Your commander guy is going to be at Eagle Falls?"

Preston gritted his teeth. It was almost painful to hope. "That's what he told Caleb."

Her arms wrapped around his waist. Her cheek rested on his back. "You're turning yourself in, and you're going to have evidence from Long that you're innocent? This is what I've been praying for."

"Me, too," he said, though he didn't have her faith. He only had a hunch that Long was on his side. If he was wrong, the trip to Eagle Falls could blow up in his face.

She laughed. "This whole time I've been kicking myself for almost marrying Caleb, but if I hadn't, we wouldn't be here right now. God can use even our mistakes for good, can't He?"

Preston reached down to cover her hand over his queasy stomach. Coming out of hiding felt much like stepping out of an airplane. Would his parachute deploy or not?

She leaned in toward his ear. "You remember the last time you took me to Eagle Falls?"

He smiled into the wind. Being with Holly unlocked all kinds of old memories. "You mean the time you pretended to see a mountain lion."

She pinched his side. "I did see a mountain lion."

"*I* didn't see a mountain lion. I think you made up the mountain lion so you had an excuse for me to hold you." That was how relationships were supposed to be. That was what theirs used to be like. Would it ever be that way again?

He looked back to find her bottom lip sticking out in a pout.

"Well, you did take forever to kiss me that first time," she said.

"I did." He'd wanted to kiss her the whole summer after their sophomore year of high school. Just didn't want to risk ruining the friendship. So he'd waited until the day they were to pack up and head home. She'd been worth the wait.

And he'd have to wait again. It was a good thing their almost kiss had been interrupted. He wasn't a free man yet. And she deserved a man free to make commitments.

Preston turned the handlebars to swing the Jet Ski around the bend into Emerald Bay and past Fannette Island, which held a few memories of its own. Maybe someday they'd get to go cliff jumping again. For now, he'd have to beach the watercraft in front of Vikingsholm, the old castle-like structure turned tourist trap. He weaved among the many boats tied to buoys and slowed to a stop.

Holly swung a leg over the seat and waded to shore. "I wish I had better hiking shoes on."

Preston looked at the small strips of leather holding the soles of her sandals to her feet. Not ideal for the upcoming trail, which included loose rock, steep stairs and a wet bridge, but they didn't have time to go shopping. He pocketed his keys and gripped her hand. "Hang on to me."

They had to move quickly. If Long's family had driven to the falls from Thunderbird Lodge, they might already be at the top by now. Preston hoped he could catch the former commander on the way back down. "If we don't find Commander Long here, we can try to find him in the Tahoe Keys."

"You know where he's staying?"

"He mentioned the big house at the end of White Sands." Preston led Holly through the trees and up a rock staircase. He looked back after her to make sure she had sure footing. She shot him a grateful smile. He'd be able to focus more fully on finding Long if she'd stop smiling at him like that.

There. He pointed past her, toward the edge of an embankment leading to a bridge. The tall, distinguished commander walked with his wife and kids. Preston's heartbeat picked up speed. "Come on."

Holly's feet slipped. She stumbled behind him. "You go." She tugged her hand from his.

Preston paused to check on her. She was fine. Just not dressed for a hike. And he didn't really need her to be part of his conversation with Long. So he'd let her rest.

Long would likely be a little shocked by his sudden appearance anyway. Probably better not to complicate things.

"Long," Preston called, jogging down the treacherous path. "Commander Long."

The man paused and looked along the walkway with a frown. His gaze focused on Preston. He blinked. Stepped backward.

Preston slowed to stop in front of the family. "Commander Long." His right hand rose to salute before he could stop himself. "I'm sorry to interrupt your vacation, sir, but I need to talk to you for a moment."

Long held a palm to his forehead. "Preston Tyler?"

The man at least recognized him. "Yes, sir."

Mrs. Long and her two teenage children stared up at him. She pointed. "Preston Tyler? As in…"

"Officer Tyler?" the teenage boy finished speaking for her. "I thought you died."

The daughter gasped.

Long placed a hand on his wife's back. "Honey, I'm going to need a moment alone with Officer Tyler."

She nodded, her jaw still slack.

Long motioned his family to keep heading toward the bridge. He stepped to the side of the path, and Preston followed after checking over his shoulder to make sure Holly was still handling the climb okay. She waved from the top of the stairs and nodded encouragingly toward his former superior.

Long clasped his hand and pumped it in a handshake. "I'm glad to see you're alive, Tyler."

The man didn't seem as stunned as his family had been. His expression remained surprisingly blank for the circumstances.

"I wish it were under better terms, sir."

"As do I."

What did that mean, coming from Long? "Sir, I've been afraid to come out of hiding because the last person I talked to was Sergeant Beatty, and the next day he ended up dead."

Long nodded. "I figured as much."

Had Long also assumed Preston was the one to kill Beatty? He pointed to his chest and shook his head. "Caleb Brooks thinks I killed Beatty, but I didn't."

Long's eyebrows drew together.

Better keep talking. "Sergeant Beatty was supposed to be looking into the sabotage I witnessed. I saw someone messing with the chopper, and I went to find him to halt the operation. I was too late."

Long nodded and looked off into the distance.

"Sir, do you know something? Because I revealed myself to Caleb, and if I don't find any evidence to support my side of the story, I could very easily end up in prison." His skin grew clammy at the thought. Not only would his life be over, but he'd be recorded in history books as responsible for the deaths of his team. His new baby nephew might someday be bullied by other kids because they'd think he was related to a traitor.

Long stuck his hands into his pockets. His wary gaze flitted over to Preston, then away again. "If anybody goes to prison, it should be me."

Preston raised his hands in a shrug. Long didn't need to take responsibility. "It's not your fault, Commander. You're not the one who—"

"Yes, I am."

Preston's chest squeezed tight against his heart as he inhaled. "What...I don't...What?"

Long looked down. "I hired a former mechanic to sabotage the helicopter to keep it from taking off."

Preston's eyes bulged. Had he heard that right?

"I didn't want anyone to get hurt. I just wanted to ground the helicopter until my brother took over as CIA director the next day. I wanted the hostage rescue to be linked to his name."

Prickles shot down Preston's arms and legs. In all his years of research, he'd never imagined this.

"When you spotted the mechanic, he got frightened and ran off, leaving debris in the engine. He must have figured you would report his tampering and the flight would be called off. When the operation continued, he ran out there to stop the pilot. He's the one whose ashes came home in your place."

Preston's body froze as his brain overloaded. And it wasn't just because Long had confessed. Or because he now knew where the man buried under his headstone had come from. But because the sabotage wasn't supposed to hurt anyone. His men had only been killed because he'd interrupted Long's plan.

Guilt roared in Preston's ears. A guilt he'd thought the truth would erase. "No," he whispered. There had to be someone else. Someone else who should be blamed for the tragedy. Another thought assaulted him. "Sergeant Beatty? Did he know of your plan? Did he actually kill himself after all?"

Long's sad eyes met his. He didn't say anything. But he didn't have to.

Preston doubled over with hands on knees as the world he knew spun violently around him. He pushed back up. He had to finish this thing. Because Caleb knew he was alive now. But, oh, what kind of defense did he have? Was Long going to admit all this to the CID? Or was it for Preston's ears only?

"Sir?" He had to ask if the commander would testify. But what did it matter? The widows of all his old friends would still look on him with scorn. He'd lived when good men had died. And they'd died because he'd lived.

He paced away to grip the rough branch of a tree, the ground still wobbly under his feet. *Help, God.* God had gotten him this far. He couldn't stop now. He strode back with purpose.

"Sir, are you willing to confess?"

Long studied him. Looked into him. Squeezed his eyes shut. "Yes, but there's more."

More? Wasn't this bad enough? Preston ran a hand over his head.

A woman's scream pierced the air. Rubble crumbled over the edge of the cliff and dust puffed up from the side of the walkway by the stairs.

Preston spun. Where was Holly? Lee stood in her place. The man lifted a boot to crush the fingers clinging to the cliff wall by his feet.

Holly.

A tsunami of blood roared through Preston's veins, deafening any warning signal that might keep Preston from charging an armed man. If Lee stepped on her hand…

He rushed forward and cocked an arm back and fired a punch before he was even aware of the intention. Lee flew backward. Preston's knuckles burned, but the pain was nothing next to what Holly must have been feeling.

"Preston."

His heart jolted at the call for help. He knelt at the edge of the trail where the rock wall plunged down to the falls below. Holly's nails clawed at the dirt, her feet pushing against a tuft of grass growing out of a small opening in the stone and tears of pain magnifying the fear in her eyes. If she fell, she might be able to slide down the steep embankment to safety. Or she might drop backward and plummet fifty feet to her death.

ELEVEN

Holly's left shoulder screamed as she squeezed her fingers over the edge of the cliff. She pressed her body closer to the cold stone. Her knuckles locked up the way they had the first time Preston taught her how to water-ski, but that memory didn't even compare to this situation. This time, if she let go, she'd be released in midair and dashed into the rocks waiting below.

Her toes curled in an attempt to dig deeper into the small patch of grass at her feet. If one foot slipped…

Her head spun. *Woe to him that is alone when he falleth.*

"Preston?" Where'd he go? He'd disappeared. Was he fighting Lee? Would Lee be able to knock him off the ledge the way he had Holly? Would Preston go flying over her head any moment? Or would his body slide into hers and bump her from her perch?

The visualizations assaulted Holly's reason. Terror churned her stomach. Why would God allow them to come this far only to abandon them to death?

"Holly." Preston's face reappeared above. He dropped onto his belly and extended an arm.

She was saved. Or was she? She could hang on with one hand and reach for Preston with the other, but where was Lee? Had Preston knocked him out? Or would he be back to attack again?

Fear held her in place. "Where's Lee?"

"Commander Long is holding him." Preston gripped her right wrist. "Can you climb up?"

Commander Long must be on their side now. That was something.

Preston grabbed her left wrist. Her shoulder throbbed. She gritted her teeth to keep from crying out.

"Now push your feet into the wall to help me drag you up."

Where was her faith? God hadn't left her alone. He wasn't going to let her fall now. With a deep breath, Holly unlocked her fingers long enough to snap them around Preston's wrists.

Her torso dropped away from the wall, but Preston held her up. Her heart thumped louder against her ribs.

Preston's teeth gritted as he strained against her weight. His eyes met hers, registered the hope. "Almost there."

Holly forced herself to breathe so she didn't pass out. She walked her feet up another inch to where she could see along the ground.

Lee's eyes met hers. He smirked. Even though he was the one being held in place by his own gun in Commander Long's hands.

She was safe, wasn't she? So why did her heartbeat halt?

Lee clenched a fist and stepped toward the older man.

"No," she shouted.

Her warning came too late. She watched helplessly as Lee knocked the gun from the older man's hands and shoved him off the side of the path and over the edge of the cliff.

Her body went limp. She might be sick.

Preston growled and gave one last yank to drag her over the edge.

She landed in the dirt and buried her face. She didn't ever want to look up again. She might have survived her fall, but Commander Long had flown too far away from the edge to grab hold the way she had.

Preston checked to make sure Lee wasn't close enough to be a threat before crawling toward the cliff. Probably to see if Long could have possibly survived. She chanced a glance at him.

He looked back at her and shook his head. Long was dead. And somehow the bad guy was still winning.

A bloodcurdling shriek pierced the air. "Robert." Long's wife raced toward them. "What did you do to my husband?"

What did *they* do? Had she not seen Lee push him off the edge?

Lee's laugh echoed from the trees. Holly turned her head in time to see him retrieve his gun from a shrub.

Preston scrambled up. He grabbed her good arm and yanked her to her feet. "Run."

Preston had to get her to the police station. He'd let authorities take it from here. He didn't want to think anymore. He didn't want to feel anymore. He didn't want to get let down by God anymore.

Had it been just last night when he'd prayed for God to avenge him of his enemies? Now the only person who could have helped him was dead. Where was the justice in that?

Worse, Holly had almost died. It would have been his fault, too. For thinking he could keep her safe and then leaving her in the hands of a murderer while he focused on his own problems.

She clutched his palm and looked around like a scared kitten on the trail back to Vikingsholm. Guests pushed past them to get to the falls and find out what was going on. Lee hadn't followed them into the crowd, but that didn't mean he wasn't waiting around the corner for his next opportunity to strike.

If only Preston could wrap his arms around Holly and tell her everything would be okay. But he didn't really believe that. And it wasn't his place. Just like it wasn't his place to call her "doll."

She climbed on the Jet Ski behind him. "Long's death isn't your fault."

He didn't argue. Because what was the point? Even if Long had survived, that wouldn't have brought any of his SOAR team back to life. The commander had lived just long enough to tell Preston how he'd played a role in their deaths.

Preston wanted to scream at God, but he needed to keep moving and watch for any more threats that would prevent Holly from getting to the police station. He turned the ignition.

Holly hugged her arms around his waist. This could be their last ride together. Their last moment alone before the press ate him alive for his involvement in the failure of Operation Desert Hope. Fitting that their relationship would end in the same place it had begun—on the lake that had once been their paradise.

He guided the Jet Ski out of the bay, wind whipping strands of Holly's hair into his face. He'd miss that feeling. His skin prickled under the sun's warmth, challenging his decision to let her go. He ignored it. It was too late now.

On autopilot, he docked the Jet Ski at Tahoe Beach Retreat. Holly showed her ID to rent bikes to ride down the trail by Lake Tahoe Boulevard. This would have made him nervous if they were still running from the cops, but they weren't. They were turning themselves in. As Preston pedaled for what might be his last bike ride ever, he couldn't ignore the memory of the first time he'd ridden down that path with Holly.

At the age of five, he'd learned to ride his two-wheeler faster than she had, and he'd raced around her while she fell and cried and climbed back on to fall again. Her dad finally gave up and told them to put their bikes in the bed of his truck so he could take them out for ice cream, which was when Preston had started to feel guilty. He'd refused to eat ice cream until she'd learned to ride her bike, too. That only made her mad. She'd climbed back onto her pink banana seat and ridden right past him to her dad's truck.

He looked back at her to find she had the same look now, the sunshine flashing across her face as she rode past trees on the forest highway. How had Caleb not fallen madly in love with her?

Her tires screeched as she squeezed her brakes and slid to a stop in the police station parking lot. "Caleb."

Had she been reading his thoughts?

She pointed. No sign of the man. Just his fancy car.

Well, they'd wanted him to go to the police, hadn't they? It was just too bad Preston hadn't gotten a chance to turn himself in before Caleb tainted his return with his version of the truth. He couldn't possibly hope the attorney had considered Preston's take on the failed operation. Or that Commander Long had ever admitted what really had happened to him.

Holly swung a leg off her bike and rolled it toward a rack. "Come on." Her voice held enough hope for both of them.

No matter what happened, he wasn't going to have to play dead anymore. He held the door open for Holly. All the fight drained out his fingertips. Was this what peace felt like? Maybe he should have handed over the reins to the investigation a long time ago. Trusted the CID to do their job.

She scanned the front room. Probably looking for Shaw. The officer would know more about her case than anyone else.

No sight of the balding man. Preston would have to look for a receptionist.

"We'll take care of Lee Galloway." Shaw cleared his throat from the other room. "Now, you say Holly Fontaine is getting help from a Preston Tyler?"

Preston paused at the sound of Shaw's gruff voice. He had no doubt who the officer was talking to. The only person who could have revealed his identity.

Holly's wide eyes darted toward the open door, where the sound of Shaw's voice had come from. She must have overheard, as well. Preston strained his ears to listen with her.

"Make no mistake, it's Preston Tyler," Caleb said. "I worked with him during Operation Desert Hope. You know, the failed hostage rescue where the helicopter crashed?"

"Yes. Go on."

The tension Preston had just released inched back into his shoulders. Holly's fingers clamped around his upper arm. Preston's troubles were only getting started.

"I suspected Tyler was responsible for sabotage, but as his body had come home in a coffin, there was really no way I could prove it. Now I know he's alive after all. I discovered my ex, Holly Fontaine, has been helping him play dead. And they just found out our former commander and the brother to the CIA director, Robert Long, is in town for the wedding. He might not be safe until Tyler is caught."

Oh no.

Holly squeaked.

"Robert Long, you say?" Shaw cursed. He must have already known about the incident at Eagle Falls.

"Dozens of witnesses will put us at the scene of the crime," Holly whispered.

Preston nodded slowly. "Including Mrs. Long, who thinks I pushed her husband."

"We have to go now." She inched backward.

He shook his head. Where would they go? Caleb had a checkmate.

She leaned forward so only he could hear her. "Hey. If I were a free woman, I could defend you in court, but Caleb just accused me of aiding and abetting. And this is a lot worse than the police suspecting I accidentally blew up a bomb in my own cabin. This is a dead military commander. Besides national attention, the government is going to demand someone be held responsible. And unless we can prove otherwise, that's going to be us."

She had a point, but he refused to take a step toward the door. This was probably pretty scary for her, but this had been his existence for a few years now.

"Holly, I've been trying to prove my innocence since the failed op, and I've got nothing to show for it." He pointed toward the exit. "If we leave now, you're risking your life on the slim chance you can uncover something I haven't."

She pulled his hand to drag him toward the door. "Not me. *We.* The both of us working together. And now that you've talked to Commander Long, we will better know where to look."

Where did she get her confidence? Maybe God just

hadn't failed her enough times to squash it yet. Though it was a little too late for God to come through. They were standing in the police station already. If they left, where would they even go?

He closed his eyes and leaned his forehead against hers. There was one place they could always get away. But to take such a risk, he would have to believe there could possibly be a reward. Maybe the reward would be nothing but spending a few more moments with her. Or maybe God really had sent her to help him.

Preston opened his eyes. Gripped her hand. At least now that Caleb had alerted Shaw about Lee, Preston wouldn't have to worry so much about the murderer, and they could focus on proving what had really happened during Operation Desert Hope. It wasn't like they could get into any more trouble than they were already in. "You've got one day." He opened the door. "Then we are coming back."

Caleb stepped out of the side room and cleared his throat, arms crossed. "In handcuffs," he added.

TWELVE

Holly's survival instinct kicked in at the sight of police officers exiting the building after them. She had to find a way to prove herself innocent so they would stop trying to arrest her. Ignoring the stinging in her shoulder, she grabbed the rental bike from the rack and ran with it so it was already rolling when she swung a leg over.

"Stop," called Shaw.

She couldn't. Because then she'd be stuck in a jail cell without the opportunity to find evidence to defend herself. If the police believed the truth, then they wouldn't be chasing her.

Back roads. Holly would dart between houses and ride through trees. The police could try to keep up, but she and Preston knew the area like they knew English. They'd grown up with it.

She whipped her head around to make sure Preston was with her before skidding off the road and down a hill. He raced just out of reach of a police officer on foot. The man in uniform turned and ran for his car.

Preston pedaled next to her. "We've got to lose them. Take a left and cut through the football field at the middle school."

Her bike bumped through grass, then up onto the

smooth surface of a running track. A cop car raced to catch up, then screeched to a halt at the fence. Gravel crunched as it reversed to race around in front of them. A siren blared.

They needed to get out of sight. "Through the baseball fields." Sweat dripped down her spine as she changed directions.

She should have gotten Preston to leave the police station sooner. Then they wouldn't have had to run from the law. Were they doing the right thing? Because if they were caught before she had a chance to get to a computer and do some research, they were going to look even guiltier.

They couldn't stop now.

Two cop cars drove along the street outside Tahoe Field. Her pulse revved like an engine and forced her to push harder on the pedals.

"We'll cut through this subdivision and the grocery store to get to the beach," Preston barked over his shoulder.

"The beach?" They needed a place to hide out where they wouldn't be spotted.

"The Jet Ski will get us to safety a lot quicker than a bike can."

As long as the police boat patrol didn't spot them.

"Okay."

Down Oak Avenue, then through a small section of woods to Treehaven Drive. A police cruiser pulled into the parking lot of the grocery store they'd been planning to cut through up ahead.

She skidded to a stop, her body jerking as if she'd hit a brick wall. Now what?

Preston motioned behind the store. They rolled the bikes down the back alley, the whir of their tires sounding loud in the silence.

Another police car screeched into the parking lot on

the other side of a gas station. Preston bolted behind a Dumpster. Holly ducked, as well. Had they been spotted?

She gulped the stale air as quietly as she could. No footsteps headed their direction. Maybe they'd made it. But they were still stuck, as Lake Tahoe Boulevard separated them from the beach. Cars whizzed past, and if Holly were to push the walk button that would clear a path for crossing, she and Preston would be discovered for sure.

She swatted at a fly intoxicated with the stench of garbage. Hiding out behind the Dumpster would only keep them safe for so long. "What now?"

Preston wiped sweat from his forehead and peeked around the corner of the building. "It looks like the police are scouting the area. If they stay here to watch for us, we're in trouble."

The bell over the gas station door chimed. Preston ducked out of sight moments before a father passed with his two laughing kids and giant ice cream cones.

Holly exhaled. What she wouldn't give to go back in time and be like those kids again.

Preston's head swiveled toward hers. "Let's get some ice cream."

She blinked at his lack of rationale. They couldn't escape into nostalgia. This trip to Tahoe was no vacation.

"I'll buy you some sunglasses and a new hat, as well."

Oh. She leaned back against the cement wall. Maybe she should *act* like she was on vacation. Police wouldn't be expecting the makeover.

She nodded. "We can leave the bikes here and wander across the street as if we don't have a care in the world." Faking nonchalance would be the challenge, but there was really no other way.

Preston peeked around the corner again. "It looks like

the officers are going to continue their search elsewhere. You ready?"

The cops were pulling out? She closed her eyes. It would be so much easier to stay in place, but if she and Preston were going to get out of there, this was their chance.

Preston slid a hand behind the small of her back to unglue her from the wall. "You go first."

Her toes tingled. Her heart thrummed. How had Preston lived like this for four years?

She rose slowly and sucked in a deep breath before stepping out into the open. No one shouted. No one pointed. No sirens blared. She could do this.

Making her way along the storefront, she craned her neck toward the convenience store windows and played with her short hair to hide her face. Finally, the entrance. She grabbed the door handle and used her peripheral vision to pinpoint the location of the employee inside. All she had to do was head directly to the sunglasses rack, and she'd have her back to him.

She swung the door open. The bell chimed. She jumped.

The man behind the counter didn't even notice. The vise grip on her heart released, with the sensation of a million pinpricks scattering down her limbs. The moment she could move again, she scampered to the back of the store.

Too bad it wasn't winter. Then she could have bought a parka and ski mask as a disguise.

The bell over the door rang again. She jerked and bumped her elbow on a shelf. But it was only Preston. She grabbed a pair of gold aviators to cover her anxiety.

"That works." Preston's reflection appeared in the tiny mirror above her face. He reached for some Ray-Bans. "Now try the woven cowgirl hat."

The bigger the hat, the more of her face she could hide. And the more she'd look like a tourist.

"Here." He grabbed the hat for her, then donned a Dodgers ball cap.

That wasn't fair. He looked just like he had in high school. Back when she couldn't take her eyes off him. Good thing she had the sunglasses to hide her gaze now. Though she should really be looking out the window to make sure they weren't in danger of being detected.

"Now ice cream?" she asked. She was ready to make their escape.

"In a sec." Preston grabbed a Styrofoam cooler and a couple bottles of water.

How much money did he have? Hopefully, enough for a sandwich and chips. She had no appetite, but she needed the energy. Who knew when they'd get another chance to eat? She ducked her head to keep from being seen by the cashier as she added the items to the counter.

Preston pulled a blue T-shirt off a hanger. It read Keep Calm and Jet Ski On. If they were going to put on all new apparel, the shirt would certainly be appropriate. She grabbed a smaller size in red, along with a pair of cheap denim shorts and flip-flops.

Preston took the tags and nodded for her to change as he paid.

Holly pulled the bathroom door closed behind her and scrambled into the stiff new clothing. She wouldn't think about what would happen once she stepped back out of the bathroom. Instead, she'd keep moving. Keep doing the next right thing. She'd slide her toes into the new shoes. Then she'd stuff the outfit she'd bought the day before into the overflowing trash can. Then she'd…

She'd stare at her reflection in the mirror. "Am I doing the right thing, Lord?"

No answer. Maybe she should pray with Preston. They used to pray together over Skype whenever he'd call her from the military. And what was that verse he used to recite? It was from Matthew 18:20. *For where two or three are gathered together in my name, there am I in the midst of them.*

Yes. They needed to pray together. They needed God's help.

She rolled her shoulders back to fake confidence before opening the bathroom door. A guy in glasses and a hat holding two ice cream cones waited for her. She blinked as a memory mixed with reality. They'd been here before. In a simpler time.

He handed her the cone. "You ready?"

She licked the sweet vanilla drip running toward her trembling fingers. In a few more licks, her tongue would go numb from the cold and not be able to taste the dessert anymore. Which could be considered symbolic of how her whole body already felt.

"I can pretend."

Preston tilted his head toward the door. "You've got me fooled."

She gave a small smile and led him, the cooler and a couple new beach towels out into the sunshine. The heat sped up the melting process on her ice cream. She continued to lick as they headed in the direction of the crosswalk. Hopefully, the treat would last long enough to hide her face until they reached the beach.

Holly pressed the button for the walk signal at the corner since Preston's arms were full. Then she ducked to take another lick of her ice cream as a different cop car pulled into the gas station parking lot. The police were everywhere. Would the officers question the store clerk this time?

Two officers climbed out of the vehicle. One began talking to customers while the second placed his hands on his hips and looked their way. Was he looking at them or past them?

Preston looped the cooler onto one elbow so he could pass his ice cream cone to the same hand and wrap the other arm around her shoulders. "Relax, Holly. Smile and flirt with me."

Flirt? Like make up a nickname for him the way he had for her and tell him how his touch made goose bumps cover her skin even on a warm day? Or maybe that was the ice cream. Or the threat of going to jail.

"You wish."

His teeth flashed in a grin. His chest bounced against her shoulder in a chuckle.

"Excuse me." An officer stepped in their direction.

Her heart rate took off like a sprinter at the sound of a starter pistol. What were they going to do now?

"I'm looking for—"

"Hey." The other cop stepped out from behind the gas station. "Young, I found something."

The bikes. Holly held her breath.

Young lifted a hand to excuse himself. The walk signal flashed to a white stick figure.

"Come on." Preston stepped into the street. "We don't want them to realize who we are until they can kick themselves for letting us get away."

Holly trotted after him, cringing in expectation of Deputy Young turning around and chasing them down. Her legs seemed to move in slow motion. Halfway there.

"Your ice cream's dripping, Holly."

Drops of cream splattered at her feet. Her fingers were covered, as well. That wasn't suspicious at all.

She stuck out her tongue to clean up the mess. First the sticky cone, then the sweet scoop. Ouch. Her temples cramped in a brain freeze.

They stepped onto the curb. Her chest heaved in relief. They'd made it. She tossed the cone into the nearest trash can and offered up a prayer of thanksgiving.

Preston stashed the small cooler underneath the Jet Ski seat. How had he ended up in this situation? Now that he was finally willing to turn himself in, he was running from more people than ever.

He looked at Holly in her silly outfit. She'd asked him to run with her. She'd asked him to give her a chance to prove them both innocent. He didn't know what she hoped to find, but he'd do anything for her. Obviously.

He scanned their surroundings one last time before climbing onto the watercraft. No uniforms on the beach yet, but police would be there soon. He'd get them out to Fannette Island before they could be followed. Then they'd have a little time to eat and rest and regroup. And pray. Because he had no idea where to go from here.

Holly scooted close and clutched his sides. "I'm not sure I can keep calm, but I'm definitely ready to Jet Ski on."

Preston turned the key. Maybe one day they'd be able to have some calm in their lives again. For the moment, he'd be thankful for a means to escape the craziness. They zipped past the resort where they'd rented the bikes and headed out into deeper water, beyond paddleboarders and a tour boat leaving the dock.

Robert Long had been ready to confess, so he might have considered Tahoe to be his last vacation before getting locked behind bars. But had he known it would lead to his death, he never would have come. Was Preston getting himself into the same situation?

He wasn't as worried about getting killed anymore now that the police knew about Lee, but if Holly didn't find evidence that Commander Long had actually hired a mechanic to sabotage the op, they would likely go to jail. This could be one of his last days riding in the wind, bouncing on the waves and burning in the sunshine. It could also be one of Holly's last days of freedom.

Preston gritted his teeth. She deserved so much more. And he'd tried so hard not to drag her into his mess.

He rounded the bend into Emerald Bay and looked back to check for police boats. All clear. Though it was definitely a lot different from the last time he'd come to Fannette Island with Holly, in search of a geocache. They'd taken a picture of themselves with the disposable camera stored in the metal lunch box behind the crumbling ruins of an old teahouse and signed their names to the notebook. The lunch box could still be there for all he knew—one of the few things that hadn't changed since his tour overseas.

Preston eased off the throttle, wishing he could slow down the guilt trip, as well. "I'm so sorry, Holly."

Her heartbeat pulsed against his back the way it used to. The way it was supposed to. The way it might never get the chance to again.

Holly pulled away as he cut the engine and glided to a stop. "What are you sorry for?"

Preston ran both hands over his head. A better question would be, what *wasn't* he sorry for? He looked into her eyes as she splashed down into the shallow water. "I'm sorry I haven't been able to come here with you for the past four years. I'm sorry we're only here now because we're hiding from police. I'm sorry you might not get to come back here for a long, long time."

"Preston." She surveyed their surroundings as if she was just as scared of being followed as he was. Then she focused on him. "You're not the bad guy here, so stop acting like it."

Was he acting like the bad guy? He certainly felt responsible for the death of his special-ops team. He'd hid out to avoid being thrown in jail. And he even kept his distance from Holly so she wouldn't get hurt. Not just Holly, though. He'd isolated himself from everyone because he was afraid his presence would bring pain to anyone involved with him.

Afraid. Holly's words from the night before roared back into his consciousness. He was afraid to love. He acted out of fear instead of love. Which was pretty much what separated the good guys from the bad guys, wasn't it?

The hard shell around his heart cracked enough for the softness inside to throb through. He didn't want it to throb. He didn't want to feel the ache that came with exposing emotion.

He swung a leg over the seat to join Holly in the water. Was this a discussion he wanted to have with her? Because it would be so much easier to give his full attention to retrieving the cooler and finding an out-of-sight place to eat than it would be to admit she'd been right about him.

But he couldn't patch the protective covering over his heart quick enough. The throb intensified as he led her into the trees and up the side of the island. He wanted to love her, but the shadow clouding their future kept him from making that move. "How do you do it? How do you believe God is going to work everything out for good?"

She stopped at the top and looked out over the cliff they used to jump from as children. "I'm afraid to not trust God."

So she had fear, too. But hers was on the other extreme. And it sounded a little like naïveté to him. "How does that work?"

"Oh, sometimes it doesn't. It's like jumping off this

rock without checking to make sure the water is deep enough first."

They both knew it was deep enough. Though Dad had still checked every year.

She sat down on a boulder. "After you didn't come home from the Middle East, I felt like God had let me down. But rather than be honest about it, I decided to be a good little Christian who never questioned Him. And that's why I didn't question Him about Caleb. I was just going to assume God's ways were better than my own and take whatever life brought me."

Preston lowered next to her. Her confession pricked his soul. And not only with knowledge that Holly had never loved Caleb. She'd broken through the bondage of complacency. She wanted more. And he wanted more for her. In fact, for the first time in a long time, he could also admit he wanted more for himself.

"But then you came back into my life, Preston," she continued. "God never let me down in the first place. And if I'd talked to Him about it and listened to His response, He probably would have kept me out of this mess we're in. So really, it's as much my fault as it is yours. And saying sorry isn't going to help anything. Whether we are here because of my blind faith or your refusal to have faith, we were both wrong. We've got to ask God for help. And we have to listen for direction. Because He knew we were going to end up here all along."

His breath caught. He stared into her clear eyes and teetered on the edge of hope. Could God possibly have brought them together for a reason? Were they created like puzzle pieces so when they worked together they could see the bigger picture of His love for them? Was this what Preston had been missing when he'd been living his life like a puzzle piece that fell off the table?

As much as he wanted to recommit to a relationship right there, they still needed to have a few more prayers answered to make it work. Their puzzle pieces didn't fit together yet.

"I really want to believe you, Holly."

She reached for his hand. "But?"

He held on despite the fact he'd soon have to let her go. "But we still aren't safe."

She studied him until he had to either look away or open up. He looked away. And when he looked back, her eyes were closed.

"Father God, Help us to trust You and Your plan for our lives. Show us where to go next. Thank You for providing this food and this moment of rest. May Your will be done. In Jesus's name, Amen."

Preston squeezed her hand before letting her go so she could eat. It was a sweet prayer, but did God care? What if it wasn't God's will to avenge his enemies?

God had allowed Lee to kill Commander Long. He'd allowed Caleb to report Preston as the possible murder suspect, not to mention the way the CID would soon be coming down on him for the sabotage of Operation Desert Hope. Preston would clarify Holly's prayer to be on the safe side. "And avenge me of mine adversary."

"Amen," Holly said again as she unwrapped her sandwich. They ate in silence, obviously both hungrier than they realized. She focused back on him after swallowing her last bite. "You don't think avenging you of your adversary is God's will?"

How did she read his mind like that? He swallowed. "It hasn't felt like it."

She twisted the top off her water and took a sip. "You went the opposite direction I did. While I decided to accept whatever came my way as God's will, you simply refused to believe God had anything good for you."

She saw it, too. He nodded at her conclusion.

"That's why we need others in our lives—to help us focus on God's truths. Like the scripture verse I was telling you about how two are better than one. When one falls, the other can lift him up."

He twisted his own bottle top open and guzzled the cool liquid to soothe his parched throat. Her words could be just as refreshing if he chose to swallow them. But how could he not? He'd seen with his own eyes how the two of them needed each other to balance out their individual flaws. They made each other stronger. Exactly the way the Bible promised. "'A threefold cord is not quickly broken.'" He quoted the verse he'd preferred to ignore.

She contemplated scripture while polishing off her bag of chips. "Are we a threefold cord?"

He wanted to be. But was God really on their side? "If God answers prayer."

Her face softened. "God brought you back to life, Preston. He can do anything."

Preston could almost believe her when he gazed into her eyes. Then his gaze shifted to the lanky man climbing up the hill behind her with a gun in his hand, and all hope was lost.

THIRTEEN

Holly followed Preston's line of sight, and she leaped to her feet. How had Lee found them again? She'd worry about that later. At the moment, they just had to get away. She reached for Preston as her feet automatically took off for the rock. They could jump...

"Stop."

Gunfire exploded. A bullet pinged off a stone only a few feet in front of her. Her heart froze along with her body.

Preston's arms wrapped around her waist and smoothly pulled her behind him. "Let her go, Lee. Caleb already went to police, so shooting her is only going to make this worse for you."

She clenched the back of Preston's T-shirt in her hands. Why was he suggesting Lee only let *her* go? She wouldn't leave him. "No—"

Preston held up a hand to silence her. She'd argue with him later. If she got a chance.

Lee frowned. "Caleb went to the police?"

She peered over Preston's shoulder. "What did you expect when Caleb took off from Thunderbird Lodge while you were chasing me with a gun?"

Lee frowned, then shook his head. "Police aren't looking for me. They're looking for you." He motioned toward them with the gun. "I saw you riding your bikes away from the cops. When you disappeared, I figured I'd check with the bike rental shop, which is where I saw you hop on your Jet Ski. Then, when I bought a ticket for a tour boat to follow you here, I overheard the police radioing the captain to ask about a couple matching your description."

Her heart sank. This would be the kind of situation that would make Preston have trouble trusting God. But she wouldn't give up. "If you kill us, they'll come after you just as hard as they're coming after us."

The gunman circled around Preston to get a better aim at her. "Come on, lawyer lady. I've already proved I'm smarter than the police. They'll think I'm a hero for catching you. Not only did the commander's wife see your boyfriend here at Eagle Falls, but I don't have a motive to kill some guy I've never met." Lee nodded toward Preston. "While I heard he does."

What had Lee heard? Did he already know Preston's identity? Was it on the local news? Possibly the national news? Holly didn't expect the government to be able to keep the press out of the story for long, but this was faster than expected. Or had the police told the captain of the tour boat what was going on, and Lee overheard that, as well?

No matter how he'd found out, he had no right to accuse Preston of a murder she'd just watched Lee commit. "How many people are you going to kill for your wife's inheritance, Lee? You're just making this worse on yourself."

Lee's eyes narrowed. "*You're* making it worse." He straightened his arm holding the gun and used his other hand to steady it for better aim.

Her pulse pounded in her ears as she watched in slow

motion. Then the back of Preston's head blocked the gun from view once again.

"Wait," he said.

No gunshot.

But her heart still leaped into her throat. Preston had been willing to play dead to keep her safe, and now he was willing to actually give his life.

She ducked under his arm to stand by his side. They were a team. She wouldn't let him face a cold-blooded killer alone.

Lee rolled his eyes. "Did you want to kiss the girl good-bye before I shoot her?"

A goodbye kiss? That couldn't be God's will for bringing Preston back into her life. No matter how hopeless Preston felt, he would never give up so easily, would he?

"Uh…yeah."

Her soul screamed. Her spastic breathing made it hard to talk as Preston turned her toward him. "Preston, you can't give up."

His hands slid to her face. His gaze bored into hers. How could his eyes seem so calm? So steady? "Holly," he whispered.

She could feel her pulse in the bottom of her feet the same way she had when he'd first kissed her all those years ago. But this was so much more. Like a first and last kiss rolled into one. Memories of their moments together faded in and out. Was this what it felt like to know you were going to die? She didn't want to die, but even more she didn't want to watch him die. "Don't give up."

"It's okay." He leaned forward. His lips were almost to hers.

Would Lee let him finish kissing her before he fired, or would one of them be killed as Preston held her? It was like that feeling at the top of the free fall ride at the amusement park when she knew she was going to plummet to the earth any second.

"I saw Caleb's boat," Preston whispered.

It took a moment to register that he wasn't whispering sweet nothings. Her fingers gripped his wrists to better block their conversation from the man watching with a gun. Was she really having a chat about her ex when their lives were on the line?

"What?"

"I'm going to attack Lee. You're going to jump off the cliff and swim to Caleb's boat."

Her toes tingled back to life. He had a plan. She could do it, except she'd need Preston by her side. And not just in case her injured arm gave out. "You jump, too."

"So one of us can get shot?"

"No," she whispered fiercely, squeezing Preston's wrists to let him know she wouldn't leave him.

"Call the police from Caleb's boat, if he hasn't already."

Her former fiancé wasn't on her side. He was on his own side. But surely she could tell him what was really going on, and he'd see how the truth could benefit him. He'd get to be the one who rescued her for all the media to see. And though he would probably be more willing to do that for her than Preston, she still wasn't going to leave Preston with a gunman as she went swimming to freedom. "I'm not going to go by myself."

"You have to." Preston glanced at her lips once more before shoving her toward the cliff and diving for Lee.

The force of his push sent her stumbling away from him against her will. She slowed her steps. Twisted. She'd run back to help him. Because two were better than one.

Preston rolled on the ground with Lee, reaching for the gun in the man's outstretched hand. The barrel arced through the air toward Holly. Gunfire blasted. The ground exploded in front of her feet.

She instinctively ducked, though Preston had taught her to duck *and* run if she was being shot at, to make herself as small a target as possible.

"Run," Preston confirmed as Lee rolled him over again. The gun slammed to the ground, still pointing her direction.

Preston said they were supposed to be a strand of three cords. That meant when she couldn't help him, God could. But she felt so alone.

She tried to comfort herself with the verse as her feet carried her toward the cliff. But it wasn't enough. Because she knew the pain of losing Preston.

A bullet zinged past her. She didn't have a choice. If she didn't leap off the rock wall into midair, he might be mourning *her* death.

She raced faster toward the spot she knew so well. Only this time there would be no giggling and hesitation in front of a waiting crowd of teenagers. She planted her foot on the last few inches of earth and bent her knee like a spring, coiled to release. She flexed through her thigh and sailed forward over the water far below.

Preston stiffened as he watched Holly disappear off the side of the cliff. But she'd be okay. She'd gotten away. That was what mattered. And now he could stop worrying about the direction the gun pointed.

Preston grunted and arched his back against the ground to flip Lee over. He rolled on top of the man and sat up.

Lee used the chance to pull his gun back in to point at Preston.

Trying to take the weapon away from a fully functioning enemy was not going to work. Preston balled his fist and smashed it into Lee's cheek.

The man's head dropped back. His arm fell to the side. The gun clattered away.

Finally. Preston scrambled after the weapon. His fingers curled around the solid handle. He pushed to his feet and spun to find Lee racing away. Though where could he go? He'd arrived by tour boat, and tour boats didn't stick around very long.

Preston would head down to his Jet Ski and be long gone by the time the police arrived. But surely they'd catch Lee.

"Freeze. Police."

Preston looked over his shoulder to find a row of cops with their guns all trained on him. Apparently Caleb hadn't waited for Holly before calling the police. He must have spotted the Jet Ski. Might have even known where to look considering Holly had probably told him all about her childhood relationship.

Preston ran his free hand over his head. Was he ever going to catch a break?

"Drop your weapon."

At least Holly was safe. Preston bent his knees slowly to place Lee's gun on the ground. He stood up and raised his arms in the air for a fraction of a second before Shaw wrenched them behind his back and snapped handcuffs on his wrists.

"You have the right to remain silent."

He'd been silent for too long. It was time he started talking. "That gun belongs to Lee Galloway. He killed Commander Long, and he was trying to kill Holly. He's the one who set the bomb at her cabin."

The cuffs tightened as Shaw turned him around for

the hike down the rock. "We know about Lee Galloway. Though it looks like he was running away from you."

Preston hung his head in exasperation. "Or he was running away from you."

Shaw nodded toward Deputy Young. "Bring Galloway in for questioning. We want both sides to this story."

If that was the best Preston could get, he'd take it.

Young holstered his gun to better traverse the hill.

Shaw pushed Preston forward. Preston glanced down to find the path, then looked back out to where Holly swam to Caleb's boat. The small figure of a man reached down to help the tiny Holly climb on board. She'd made it safely despite her bullet wound. Maybe everything would work out after all.

"Hey," Young shouted.

Preston returned his attention to the drama below. Lee shoved his way past the deputy, toward Preston's Jet Ski. Had the man grabbed his keys in the scuffle? And now he was going to escape on Preston's own watercraft?

Shaw released Preston and stepped next to him, aiming his gun down at the other man. "Stop. You're under arrest."

But Lee didn't stop. He swung a leg over the seat and turned the ignition.

If he got away, Holly's life could still be in danger. Would Lee ride out to Caleb's cabin cruiser and kill her right there? It wouldn't be good for his case, but neither was running from the cops. The man was desperate. And he might be out for revenge.

Every muscle in Preston's body tensed. If he wasn't handcuffed, he would run and jump off the cliff himself so he could swim out to save Holly.

Fire leaped from Preston's Jet Ski. Lee disappeared in the explosion that echoed through the bay. The ground shook. Pieces and parts of the watercraft rained down into the lake. The stench of charcoal and burning plastic permeated the air.

Deputy Young leaped away from the flames, covering his face. Other officers shouted and ran to help. But Preston stood in shock, staring at what must have been the results of a bomb.

The bomb was on his Jet Ski, so it had been planted for him. But if Lee planted it, why would he set it off? Could he have simply forgotten he'd put it there? No. Because if Lee had planted it in the first place, he wouldn't need to go after them with a gun. He could have simply let them die in the blast.

Preston couldn't breathe. And not just because of the smoke in the air. But because there had to be another killer who'd set the bomb.

Hadn't Commander Long told him there was something else? Could Lee have had a motive to kill Long after all? To hide what he knew? But Lee hadn't been involved in the sabotage on Operation Desert Hope.

Preston turned his head toward the cabin cruiser. Caleb.

Caleb had been the JAG lawyer who'd proven the helicopter explosion to be an accident even though he'd said he suspected sabotage. What if he'd known about Long's involvement and blackmailed the Commander? Or maybe Long had hired him to help cover it up. And what if Beatty hadn't really killed himself after all? Could Caleb have hanged him?

That meant he'd known Preston was innocent from the beginning. He'd used Holly as bait to track him down to silence him for good.

That was where Lee came in. He wasn't after Holly because Caleb refused to represent him. No, Caleb must have agreed to represent him if he killed Preston and Holly. If

Lee had let Caleb know he'd tracked them to the island, then Caleb could have followed and set the bomb to kill Lee after Lee killed Preston and Holly, covering all his tracks.

And the whole time they'd been trying to warn Caleb away from the hit man he'd hired.

"No," Preston shouted, lunging toward the unveiled enemy who now had Holly in his clutches.

Shaw spun back to contain him.

Preston shouldered him away to push past. "Holly! Get off the boat."

Shaw's baton smashed into the back of his knee.

Preston ignored the throbbing pain pulsing down his calf and stumbled forward. "Holly, get away. You have to swim."

A large body smashed into Preston from behind. He crashed down onto the rock without his hands to stop the fall. His chest hit first. He strained his neck to keep his face from connecting with stone. But Shaw jumped onto his back and pressed his head toward the ground.

Preston twisted to stare out at the water below—at what could have been a peaceful scene of a boat floating on the water had he not just sent Holly into the center of a whirl-pool. There was no way to rescue her now.

FOURTEEN

Holly let go of her throbbing shoulder to cover her mouth. Had she really just seen the Jet Ski explode with Lee on it? At least it hadn't been Preston. Because it very well could have been. Ironically, she was thankful Caleb had called the police soon enough to detain Preston and keep him from falling into Lee's trap.

Wait. Lee couldn't have set that bomb. If he had, he never would have gotten on the Jet Ski.

Denise sobbed silently next to her on board the deck.

Holly stepped away and studied her warily. Could the woman have set the explosion for Holly? And now she felt bad for killing someone else? But if her goal had been to kill Holly, why had she let Caleb help her on board?

Caleb blew out a big breath and stepped between the women. "I never would have expected Preston to go this far," he said.

Holly rubbed her trembling arms to heat up. At least she wasn't alone. But what was going on? Lee had just been blown up… Preston had been arrested…

It took a moment for Caleb's words to register. He hadn't expected Preston to go this far? "What do you mean?" She studied his cavalier expression.

Caleb motioned to the beach. "Preston blew up Lee."

Holly's jaw dropped. How could he make that statement with such certainty? His convincing tone almost had her doubting Preston, though she'd been with him the whole time they'd been at the island.

"That makes no sense."

Caleb crossed his arms and turned to face her, the cold glint in his eyes causing her to shiver even more. "Make no mistake, that's what Shaw is going to believe. You should have seen him salivate when I told him there was an old SOAR pilot playing dead in his jurisdiction."

Dread clutched her like a giant claw. Why was Caleb doing this? "You went to the police to tell them Lee Galloway was after me because I'd convinced you to drop his case, right?"

"Of course." Caleb chuckled. "Though Lee Galloway was actually after you because I agreed to take his case only if he took care of you like he did his wife. It's a pity he didn't finish the job before I had to get rid of him. I was sure he had you here."

Holly's heart jumped in her chest, knocking her backward. She stumbled into the cabin wall behind her. How had she ever thought she could marry this monster? "You wanted him to kill me because I broke off our engagement?"

Caleb smirked over at Denise as if she were part of an inside joke. "Hardly. You already know you were a pawn to bring Preston out of hiding. He didn't reveal himself the way I thought he would, but who else would have sent you those photos? You suspected Denise. I knew better."

Holly's gaze slid to the other woman. Was this the plan she'd spoken about so casually at Thunderbird Lodge? Denise wouldn't even make eye contact.

"I hired Galloway to raise the stakes, and it worked like a charm."

Caleb had wanted [—]
been willing to kill her [—]
click. She inched sideway[—]
Lee keep trying to kill me [—]
at Thunderbird Lodge? Why [—]
lice to arrest Preston?"

Caleb waved his hand as if h[—]
ter. "I didn't want to prosecute [—]
dead. See, Commander Long paid [—] me to
cover his mistake up during Operati[—] Hope, and
I couldn't let anyone find out."

Thoughts raced. Images. Memories, really. That made
all the pieces fall into place. And froze her blood. Caleb
was pure evil. But how did he think he could win this?
Did he still plan to kill her?

She pointed toward the island where Officer Shaw was
wrestling Preston on board the police boat. "Preston is in
police custody, and he's going to tell them everything."

Caleb stroked his chin. "Yeah, that wasn't part of my
plan. Someone else must have seen Lee on the island with
a gun and alerted police. But look at the way Preston's
fighting authorities. I'm pretty sure that no matter what
he says, I'm still going to be able to make a pretty good
case against him."

She didn't want to believe it, but Preston was acting
like a lunatic, knocking men over as the police hauled
him onto the boat. What had gotten into him? He needed
Shaw on his side.

Unless Preston had figured out Caleb had been the one
to set the bomb for Lee. He was trying to warn her. But
what could she do? They'd been a team. She wouldn't be
able to overpower Caleb and Denise on her own.

Caleb pulled his cell phone from his pocket and di-
aled. "Officer Shaw, it looks like you've got your hands

e care of Tyler. I will meet you at
ly."

eb was the one who'd been trying to kill her
e very beginning. She reached for the phone. "Of-
er Shaw—"

"You're welcome, sir." Caleb pressed the end button.

Holly yanked her hand away, but she couldn't keep it from shaking. The trembling radiated from her very core like she could feel the vibrations of the police boat as it started its engine and jetted away. "You're not going to take me to the dock like you said, are you?"

Caleb winked. "You're going to go for a swim, sweetheart."

A swim? Her breath caught. Normally that wouldn't be so bad. But if Caleb dumped her in the middle of the lake, there was no way she could get to shore with her injury. She'd drown. Or worse, get run over by a boat.

If she was going to go for a swim and survive, she'd have to do it here. Holly charged toward the water.

Caleb caught her and shoved her back against the cabin and out of the line of sight from police. She opened her mouth to yell. Something hard and small poked into her belly.

A gun? Caleb had his own gun?

Her chest heaved as she fought to hold in her scream. She stared up into Caleb's solemn eyes. She'd have a better chance of survival if he left her to drown. Though if he shot her, it would be harder for him to pin all his crimes on Preston.

"Don't make me shoot you in self-defense." He always had an excuse.

What did she do? *Help, Lord.*

A bright red shape rose behind Caleb's head. It clanked

down against his skull, knocking him overboard. He thrashed in the water and tried to swim toward the boat.

Holly sucked in a gulp of fresh oxygen and stared at Denise holding a fire extinguisher.

"I'm the one who called the police," Denise said through tears. "He said he was going to help you out, and I didn't realize he was setting a bomb on your boyfriend's Jet Ski. I may not be a good person, but I would never kill anybody."

Holly reached for the other woman and gave her a shaky hug. She'd once thought this woman was behind the bomb and hit man. "You...you saved my life."

Denise squeezed back, then wiped her nose to compose herself. She stepped out of Holly's embrace and strode to the helm. "We better get away from Caleb if we want to stay alive."

Holly nodded, still a little speechless. She hung on to the railing as Denise gunned the motor. Caleb remained treading water behind them. He punched the air and yelled something, but Holly was relieved not to be able to hear over the engine.

A second police boat pulled into the bay. She'd let the law enforcement retrieve Caleb from the water. He'd still lie to them, but he wouldn't be able to hurt anyone else.

"Want me to take you to South Tahoe Police Department?" Denise asked.

Holly nodded and closed her eyes. Preston's fear of going to jail might soon come true. If nothing else, he'd be in big trouble for resisting arrest. It was too bad nobody else could corroborate their story of Commander Long's cover-up.

But what if there was someone? Someone who would want Caleb to go to jail for murder as badly as she did? Someone like Commander Long's wife?

"Denise." She pressed forward through the wind to join the other woman. "Take me to the Tahoe Keys. There's someone I think we should take to STPD with us."

Denise nodded numbly. Finding out her boyfriend was a killer had to be a lot to take in by itself. Holly let her process it. While she processed Preston's defense.

She'd wanted a chance to get back on the internet to do more research. Maybe now was the time. On Caleb's boat of all places. "You get me across the lake as quickly as possible. I'm going to use Caleb's computer in the cabin."

Holly rushed down the stairs and snapped open Caleb's laptop as the boat jerked forward. She righted herself enough to run an internet search: Operation Desert Hope.

She scrolled through articles, scanning for whatever it was that had jumped out at her the day before in the business office of Cedar Glen lodge. But she'd read these articles many times after Preston's supposed death, and she hadn't caught anything then. What made her think she could catch something now?

The black-and-white photo of a burning helicopter popped onto the screen. The same image she'd seen at the lodge. Now that she knew who'd caused the explosion, could she prove it?

This was her job. What she got paid big bucks to do. She leaned forward and narrowed her eyes to block out all emotions from the past day. What could she use in a court case? Her focus dipped down to the article.

Eight soldiers were killed in military helicopter explosion in Afghanistan when chopper crashed into fuel tanker. Officials say the crash was caused by pebbles and gravel in the engine, and though the debris allowed the helicopter to take off, it later traveled into the gearbox and cut power. There is no

foul play suspected at this time, though Commander
Robert Long plans to investigate the negligence re-
sulting in such a tragedy.

None of that told her anything new. In fact, it was in-
accurate. Yes, there had been eight men, but where had the
eighth man come from? If it wasn't Preston, who was it?

Perhaps the evidence wasn't in the stories about the
crash. What if there was something in a related story that
Preston wouldn't have known was related until now. She
pulled up the full newspaper from the same day.

Some text buried at the bottom of page six caught her
eye.

Investigators search for Sergeant Matthew Hayes, a
US soldier who deserted his post in Afghanistan earlier today. Commander Long suspects he has been
taken captive by the enemy, and they will soon receive an offer for prisoner trade.

Holly slammed back into her seat at the sight of Commander Long's name in print. Had Matthew Hayes ever
been found? Or had he been sent back to the States in
Preston's coffin?

Her belly warmed in disbelief of the coincidence. She
held her breath and typed the missing soldier's name into
the search engine.

Sergeant Matthew Hayes still missing.

Foreign government denies capture of Sergeant
Matthew Hayes.

Family of Sergeant Matthew Hayes refuses to
believe he deserted the military.

Holly shook her head. Those poor parents. Probably still hoping for their son to return. They deserved some closure. Even if it hurt for them to hear their son accepted payment from Commander Long to sabotage the helicopter and had accidentally caused the death of the troops involved with Operation Desert Hope, they would finally have answers. They could have a proper funeral.

That was, if Holly was right. She'd share her suspicions with Mrs. Long. The woman wouldn't be aware of military operations, but she'd known her husband. She'd have known about Sergeant Hayes. She'd have known how Commander Long reacted to the man's disappearance. And surely she'd see the connection.

Preston had never suspected Commander Long of sabotaging his own crew, so he wouldn't have considered the man would cover up the sergeant's disappearance. But now it all fit. And once Mrs. Long realized Caleb had had her husband killed, she'd realize Preston and Holly were on her side. Then, Holly hoped, she'd be on theirs.

Preston held his wrists close together so the handcuffs wouldn't tighten from resistance as the police boat bounced over the waves, though his heart throbbed against his chest as if trying to go after Holly by itself. He stared back at the cove as it grew smaller in the distance.

A body had flown out of the *Knot Guilty*. Too big to be either Holly or Denise. Had Holly really overpowered her ex? The cabin cruiser had then zipped away, leaving the killer floating in its wake.

Preston relaxed back into his seat. This was it. The end of his life. A strange peace poured over him as the boat headed across the lake.

He watched as a second police boat picked up Caleb.

Preston exhaled. Even if police still thought Caleb was the good guy, they had him in their custody.

Except the other boat veered after the *Knot Guilty*. No way. The dirty attorney was using a police escort to chase down Holly?

Preston bolted to his feet. "Where are they going?"

He had to be wrong. Shaw would surely have some explanation that made more sense.

The officer cleared his throat. "Police are tracking down your accomplice, of course. It looks like she stole Mr. Brooks's boat."

If Caleb had the police taking him to find Holly, then what hope was there? Nobody was safe. Unless Preston could convince Shaw to get the other boat to bring Caleb in.

Preston growled and pulled against the cuffs. "No. She didn't steal Caleb's boat. She's trying to get away from him."

Shaw chewed on a fingernail. "Mr. Brooks isn't the bomber. We already checked his alibi for when the Fontaine cabin exploded."

"I know." Preston implored the lawman with his eyes. "Caleb hired his client Lee Galloway to set the bomb. Then Caleb killed him with one of his own bombs. And now Caleb is going after Holly because she knows I'm innocent."

Shaw narrowed his eyes. "But why would Brooks commit all those crimes in the first place? You're the one who's been hiding from the government for four years after sabotaging Operation Desert Hope."

This was why Preston had never turned himself in to begin with. He'd already been framed so well that he might as well smile and say cheese. But now his innocence mattered more than ever. Because it was convincing the authorities of his innocence that would save Holly's life.

"No. I didn't." He explained everything he'd discovered with the sabotage of Operation Desert Hope.

Shaw traded looks with the officer behind the wheel. "We have a witness who says you killed Commander Long, you know."

Preston closed his eyes. One more person he hadn't been able to get to fast enough. "I know."

"I suppose Brooks had Long killed, too?" The officer didn't have to sound so mocking.

Preston's heart sank. Why was this happening? Why was he in handcuffs while the real killer was free to hunt down Holly? *Why, God?* He'd been right not to hope. God obviously didn't care about justice the way the Bible said. He turned away from Shaw and stared straight ahead. "Yes."

"And Brooks somehow framed you?"

Preston flicked Shaw a glance. Why even ask questions if he wasn't going to listen? Preston would respond for the same reason he'd quit tugging on his handcuffs—to keep from making his situation worse. It wasn't like either Shaw or the handcuffs would be letting him go.

"Holly and I went to Eagle Falls to talk to Commander Long. I was with him when Lee Galloway pushed Holly over the edge. I was pulling Holly back up when Lee knocked the commander off the cliff. Lee had a gun, so we ran."

Shaw rubbed his nose. "Interesting that out of all the tourists there, you are the only ones who saw Lee."

Preston locked his jaw. There was nothing interesting about pulling Holly back up the cliff she'd been pushed off and being only an arm's length away from her as she watched death take a life for the very first time. It had been another reminder of how he couldn't win. Kind of like now.

"Well, Tyler." Shaw clapped his hands together. "I find your story worth looking into, though I'm not going to be the one looking into it. Because of Commander Long's death, the Army Criminal Investigation Division Command—or the CID as you probably know them—are at the dock, waiting to take you into custody."

Holly raced up the stairs to the deck of Caleb's boat with a printed copy of the newspaper article. She had to get the evidence in front of Mrs. Long so she could back up her story. Holly didn't want to be insensitive to the woman's grief, but knowing the truth might actually help the woman heal.

Denise stood at the helm, slowing the throttle as they neared the entrance to the private marina community. Her hair floated down to her shoulders as the wind died.

Holly looked past her, toward the canals lined with docks and decks. Preston had said Long was staying at the end of White Sands, so that was the first peninsula on the left. She pointed to the largest home. "There."

Denise cranked the wheel to pull the direction Holly had pointed. "Holly, I'm so sorry. For everything. I seriously thought Caleb was after some kind of terrorist and you were in on it. I didn't…I didn't realize…" She sniffed and wiped her wet cheek.

Holly shook her head. Denise wasn't the only one who should be sorry. She put a hand on the woman's warm, smooth shoulder. "I'm sorry, too. When this all started, I thought you were the one trying to kill me out of jealousy."

Denise blinked, her clear eyes shining with innocence. "No. I…I…"

"You made some poor choices, but in the end, you got

fooled by Caleb just like I did. It's never too late for re-demption."

The woman looked down for a moment before focus-ing on the dock she needed to steer beside. "I don't know what I'm going to do now. Caleb has always taken care of me financially. All I've had to do was look pretty and dote on him. I don't have any job skills. I don't—"

"You could be my assistant." The words popped out before Holly had a chance to measure their weight. She pondered the idea as she reached over the side of the boat to catch the dock. Maybe it wasn't a bad idea. If she was going to start her own law firm, she'd definitely have to do some hiring.

Denise turned off the engine and cocked her head. "You'd hire me? After all this?"

Crazy how life worked out. *If* it worked out. "Only if I'm not sent to prison and still allowed to keep my law li-cense. You saved my life, Denise."

Holly turned from Denise to scan the area. Wow. The place had to be four times the size of Holly's old cabin. Would Mrs. Long even hear her knock on the door?

"Come on. We'll find Mrs. Long and explain what's going on." She placed her hands on the edge of the smooth fiberglass boat and vaulted over it onto the dock.

"Wait. Holly?"

Holly didn't have time to wait. She looked over her shoulder as she jogged along the faux-wood planks.

"Caleb's coming."

Adrenaline shot down Holly's spine. She had to move fast. Though she didn't see Caleb, she saw a police boat growing larger as it neared them. But the police wouldn't let Caleb do anything to them.

"It's going to be okay. Just come help me—"

The cabin cruiser's motor revved back to life. "Caleb

might kill me if I talk to police," Denise yelled back. "I have to go."

"No." Holly held out a hand to stop her, but it was too late.

Denise pulled away to turn the *Knot Guilty* around and squeeze past the police boat. Would the police follow her or keep tracking down Holly? She ducked behind a shed in hopes they would continue after the boat. She needed Denise to talk to police.

She also needed to speak with Mrs. Long alone. The woman would probably handle the revelation of her husband's sabotage better if it was done discreetly rather than in front of an audience of cops.

The police boat pulled around the dock to back up and turn around. The officers focused on the *Knot Guilty* as one barked at the driver through a bullhorn to shut down her craft. Denise kept going.

Caleb looked Holly's direction. He moved toward the side of the boat and yelled over the sound of the engine, "I think Holly let Denise go. Let me off here with my girlfriend, and you can track down Preston's partner."

Denise? He'd said she was Denise?

Unbelievable. Did the man ever tell the truth? Caleb was sending police after the other woman so he could come after Holly himself.

FIFTEEN

The police wouldn't really listen to Caleb, would they? They were in the middle of a police investigation. Even if they believed Caleb's girlfriend had just been released from a dangerous boat thief, they wouldn't slow the boat to drop him off. Right?

Caleb leaped over the side of the boat and saluted as the police vessel sloshed away. Oh no. Should Holly run out onto the dock and call the police back for help before they were out of sight? But if she didn't make it in time, she'd be facing off with a murderer alone. She'd be better off if she kept going and put space between her and Caleb.

She raced up the hill along the side of the house to knock on the front door. No Caleb in sight.

She didn't have time for hide-and-seek with the enemy. Pressing the doorbell, she willed Mrs. Long to be home. No footsteps. No dog barking. Nothing.

Holly pounded her fist against the wood. Was the woman making funeral arrangements elsewhere, or was she mourning quietly inside? She must have been elsewhere. Because surely her teenage children would come to the door if they were there.

Plan B. Holly had to get to a safe place. Maybe the neighbors would let her use their phone to call the police.

She slowed her pace. First, she'd figure out where Caleb had gone so she could wait until he was looking the other way and race across the property. Creeping to the side of the house, she prepared to peek around the corner.

Keep me safe, Lord. She took a deep breath before leaning forward.

Thunk.

Lightning zigzagged through her skull and all sound faded. She reached out for reality. What had happened? An intense pounding in her skull dimmed her vision with every throb. Caleb appeared in her narrowing line of sight, a wicked grin on his face, a shovel in his hands.

She reached to stop him but caught nothing. She stepped but found no footing. Then the world faded…except for the pungent smell of gasoline.

Preston watched as the town grew closer. Would this be his last ride on the lake ever? He closed his eyes and took a deep breath of the fresh mountain air. He sniffed again. That didn't smell right. Smoke?

He opened his eyes and scanned the mountains. A little early for wildfires, wasn't it? No large gray puffs of smoke signaled such a disaster. He looked out across the lake. The sky seemed pretty clear on that side, as well. Maybe someone was just barbecuing. Someone who burned everything he put on the grill like Holly's dad did.

Holly. Preston jerked as a thought assaulted him. No… it couldn't be. Caleb wouldn't be able to do anything to her with the police watching.

He jumped to his feet and scanned the shoreline anyway. A small puff of smoke billowed from the direction of the Tahoe Keys. Where he'd told Holly the Long family was staying.

His skin crawled. He yanked at the cuffs. The metal

bands wrapped tighter around his wrists, but the pinch barely registered. He yanked again in anger at his powerlessness. What was he going to do?

"Sit down, kid. You have nothing to worry about. Even if Caleb is as dangerous as you say he is, he's with another officer. Nothing bad is going to happen."

Nothing bad? Everything was bad, but nobody believed him. "There's a fire."

Shaw shrugged. "Probably a barbecue."

"No. There's a fire." Preston pushed toward the end of the police boat for a better view as it pulled into the dock. "Radio your other boat. See if Caleb is still on it."

There was nobody else after them, was there? Caleb had killed both Lee and Long. And he was probably on the other police boat. Which meant Preston was just being paranoid.

Shaw scratched his head but picked up his radio. Another officer gripped Preston's arm to walk him toward the dock. Preston strained to hear the conversation behind him. If Caleb had somehow gotten away from the police, Preston would have to convince Shaw to check out the Keys.

"Preston Tyler." A graying man in a brown suit greeted him from the dock. "You are under investigation for the murder of former SOAR Commander Robert Long."

Preston gave him a quick glance. "I didn't do it."

They'd most likely get to know each other really well, but at the moment their relationship was the least of Preston's concerns. Shaw knew what was going on. Shaw was the one who could help him.

Shaw pressed the button on his radio. "Shaw here. Is Brooks still with you on your boat?"

Static crackled. A tinny voice responded, "Brooks got

off at a cabin in the Tahoe Keys to help his girlfriend. We are currently in pursuit of Fontaine driving Brooks's boat."

"No." That couldn't be right. Preston shook his head and pulled away from the officer who held him. Fear welled like a tsunami in his heart, ready to crush anything in its path. "Robert Long was staying in the Tahoe Keys. If anybody got off there, it was Holly. She'd want to talk to Long's wife to help prove me innocent."

Shaw's eyes flicked Preston's direction, uncertainty darkening their depths. "Ten-four," he said into the receiver before setting it down.

"Long's wife?" The suit repeated Preston's words. Maybe he would help. "If anything happens to Mrs. Long…"

The man was threatening him? How could the CID be so backward? Preston rushed toward the dock to plead his case.

Something hard rammed into the back of Preston's knees. Stupid police baton again. He buckled for a moment but caught himself. Or maybe the other officer's grip on his arms was what caught him.

The man on the dock reached inside his suit jacket as if grabbing a gun from his shoulder holster to protect himself. How had Caleb gotten them to believe he wasn't the dangerous one?

Shaw. He was the only one who'd even considered what Preston had to say.

He craned his neck to beg over his shoulder, "Send them back. Send the other boat back to check it out."

Shaw shook his head, but his lips pressed together in thought. "They are in pursuit of a suspect we believe to be your accomplice. I can't halt the chase because you tell me to."

"They're chasing the wrong person." Preston's feet

dragged against the deck as the officer behind him pulled him away. He bent his bruised knees to plant himself in the spot. "Your deputies released a man very capable of murder, and now there's a fire. Those are facts, not my advice."

Panic rose in his throat to choke him. He'd seen what fire could do. He'd seen the charred remains, known the people whose lives had disintegrated into nothing, been troubled by memories of what once had been—what should have been. His reality would soon be a memory. The woman he'd longed to hold in his arms wouldn't even have a body after the fire. Her spirit of hope and the resolve that made the world a better place would have vanished.

"I'll send a fire truck." Shaw picked up the receiver again.

Preston swallowed down the terror as best he could. The firemen would do their jobs. They'd rescue anybody trapped in Long's vacation rental. They'd put out the flames before the heat could suffocate Holly with smoke. Because if they didn't...

The scent of burning wood swirled about him, smothering him with hopelessness and at the same time igniting a determination within. Preston couldn't just climb onto the dock and stand there as the deputy unsnapped one of the handcuffs behind Preston's back only to reattach it to the CID detective's arm. If they weren't going to do something, he would. And this was his chance. But what could he do? *What, Lord?*

The sound of whipping wind drew Preston's attention. He knew that sound well. A familiar Robinson R44 warmed up its propeller from a helipad above the water. Hank, the old man from down the street. He'd already done so much for Preston. Would he be willing to help save Holly, as well?

The soles of Preston's feet itched. He couldn't stay still. He couldn't leave Holly to deal with attempted murder when there was something he could do about it. Even if it got him in more trouble later. The only thing worse than spending a lifetime in prison would be spending a lifetime in prison feeling responsible for another death.

The man in the suit held out his arm to have the other half of Preston's handcuffs snapped on by Shaw's deputy. He was doing his job and wouldn't understand Preston's desperation. He'd probably pull his gun and shoot. Maybe Preston would get a chance to explain one day. Maybe not. He met the man's steely gaze. "I'm sorry."

The man lifted his chin, then his eyebrows. "Are you confessing?"

"No. I'm leaving." Preston yanked his arm away to rip the handcuffs from the police deputy and charged toward the ladder that would take him to the helipad. He leaped before reaching it and grabbed the highest rung he could. He tucked his abs in to yank his feet up.

"Stop him," Shaw barked from behind.

It would take a bullet to stop him. But no bullets whizzed by.

Feet pounded on hardwood. The ladder shook as someone reached it below. But they mercifully hadn't fired any guns. Probably mercy for the tourists climbing aboard the chopper, not for him.

He hoisted himself to the top of the pad and pushed through the wind toward the pilot. "Hank, I need a lift to the Tahoe Keys. There's a cabin on fire, and a friend of mine may be inside."

The pilot's helmet turned so Preston could make out a ruddy face and crazy eyebrows. "Preston? You want me to fly you to the Keys to rescue someone?" His jowls jiggled as he grinned. "I knew there was more to you than an antisocial recluse."

If that was a vote of confidence, he'd take it. "I'm a former SOAR pilot framed for sabotage." He leaped into the empty passenger seat. "I was going to turn myself in, but I've got to save someone first."

Hank nodded. "A woman?"

"Yes." He'd let Hank assume anything he wanted about his relationship to the woman if it got him to her faster. "Fly me over the lake, and I'll jump out in the canal when we get close." His gut churned at the thought of what Holly might be experiencing at that very moment.

Hank slammed his door closed and motioned for Preston to do the same. "Buckle up, folks." He nodded toward the couple in the backseat. "SOAR started after I flew choppers for the military, but that's not going to keep me from helping out a fellow vet now."

Shaw's deputy and the CID officer waved arms overhead from the edge of helipad as Hank pulled the collective back and lifted the throttle to raise the chopper into the air.

The man in the backseat pointed out the window. "I think the police want you to go back down, sir."

"Oh my." The wife gasped and stared at the handcuff hanging from Preston's right wrist. "He's wearing handcuffs."

The R44 tilted to one side as Hank turned them around. Preston twisted against gravity to comfort the passengers. "Ma'am, the man who killed my military commander is likely trying to kill my...my...childhood sweetheart." No more assumptions. Now everyone knew how much Holly meant to him.

The woman in the backseat leaned forward. "You're trying to save your sweetheart?"

Would she ever be his sweetheart again? She might if he got there in time. "Yes, I am."

The woman's tiny hand reached up and slapped Hank's shoulder. "Fly faster."

"Roger."

The column of smoke grew larger. Preston's own lungs burned as his gaze followed the trail down to the large house just past the opening to the Keys. Flames danced on the roof. Why couldn't he have been wrong?

Preston unsnapped his seat belt. He wouldn't ask Hank to land. All the wind from the propellers could easily cause the fire to spread. Plus he had to get down there immediately. Had to know for sure if Holly was inside. He gripped the door latch and scanned the narrow waterway for the best position from which to jump.

"I'll hover out past the dock." Hank lowered toward the canal before balancing the collective, cyclic and tail rotor. Water churned beneath them, licking up whitecaps. If only they had a helicopter bucket to pick up water from the lake and dump it on the cabin. "Ready?"

Preston took a deep breath and looked over to the cabin one more time. *God, if You care...*

A man stepped out from behind the shed and raised his arm. Caleb with a gun.

Preston jolted in surprise, then continued the movement to dive toward Hank and shield him with his body. "Get down," he yelled to the couple in back.

Why hadn't he expected this? Maybe because the attorney would have a tough time explaining his reason for shooting at a helicopter tour. There would be witnesses. Unless he killed them all to keep his act going. Or did he think he could somehow spin this? Claim he thought Preston had set the fire and was trying to get away?

A gunshot rang in the air. A bullet zinged through the

window. Air pressure tugged at Preston's eardrums, the rotary blades whirred louder, the helicopter tipped side to side, and the woman behind him screamed, but at least nobody had been—

Something wet trickled over Preston's hand where he'd reached across the pilot to shield him.

Hank moaned and gripped his chest. "Think I'm gonna have myself a fine scar, folks."

Blood oozed through Hank's fingers down onto Preston. The pilot had been shot.

SIXTEEN

Preston ducked as another bullet shattered glass this time. Wind whipped through the open window. Even if Hank could still fly, there was no way the chopper would make it back to the helipad. Preston wouldn't be jumping out of the helicopter. He'd be landing it.

"Hank, trade me places." He'd been helpless for so long. But not now. Now once he got the cyclic between his legs and the tail rotor pedals at his feet. And all Caleb had was a gun? The criminal better watch out.

Hank reached for the seat belt slowly. Too slowly.

"Come on, Hank," Preston urged.

The man nodded, his jowls flapping. But he didn't seem to have the power to respond any more than that. Hank needed help.

Another bullet pinged against metal.

Preston's heart lodged in his throat. As if in reflex, he unstrapped Hank's seat belt and pulled him to his lap in the passenger seat.

The woman in the back shrieked when she got a glimpse of Hank's chest wound.

"I'm okay," Hank murmured. "I'm…" He sank, unconscious, to the floor.

The chopper tilted left. The woman screamed again.

Preston let the force of gravity pull him over into the pilot's seat. He gripped his harness to connect the straps. He now had to land not only to get to Holly but to get medical attention for Hank.

A fourth slug sliced through the air and dived into the back of Hank's seat. If the man hadn't been slouched forward, he would have been hit a second time.

That was it. Preston pulled the nose up slightly to get them out of Caleb's line of sight. The position would also help keep his forward movement slow enough to land in the cul-de-sac on the other side of the house. It wasn't going to be easy to land the chopper from a hover, but Preston didn't have many choices. He shifted the collective and eased over the roof toward cement.

Caleb appeared below him again, ducking behind a house next door.

Preston armed the parking brake, reduced momentum, leveled altitude and adjusted the collective. The helicopter jerked to a landing, jarring his teeth and rocking Hank's head back.

Ripping the first aid kit from the ceiling, Preston dug for gauze to press against Hank's wound. "Hold this," he ordered the man behind him to lean forward and take over. "And you call 911," he said to the woman. They scurried to comply though if Shaw had anything to do with it, they would already be on their way.

Preston scanned the area for Caleb before swinging the door open and leaping to the ground. No sign of the other man. Preston raced across the lawn toward the front door. A wall of heat washed over him, but he refused to slow. A shovel lay at the doorstep. A weapon? Preston tensed even more as he stepped over the tool. "Holly?" He coughed at the liquid-like smoke threatening to drown him.

A bright red T-shirt drew his eyes toward the floor by

the couch, reminding him of the way he'd hid with her behind a couch the day before. Why hadn't he taken her suggestion and revealed himself then? They could have avoided all this—avoided the question as to whether she was even alive or not.

He dived to his hands and knees to get below the smoke and pulled the soft neckline of his tee over his nose and mouth to use as a mask. Holding his breath, he crawled across the floor. He gripped Holly's shoulder to shake her awake. Her face rolled to the side. Her beautiful face. No response. But her chest rose and fell rhythmically, signifying she was still alive. He had to get her out of there to keep her that way.

The front door slammed shut behind him, caging the smoke and forcing it to sink lower over his head. Caleb. The man must have waited for him to enter and probably barred the door with the shovel.

Sweat rolled down Preston's nose, though the heat of the fire wasn't nearly as bad as the burning in his lungs. And Holly had been breathing the smoke in much longer than he had.

Fear clawed at his heart. Not fear of Caleb anymore. But fear of losing the most important person in his life. Even when he'd had no life.

Was she lying under blankets? So heavy. So hot. She needed to kick them off. And she needed a drink. Her throat burned like she'd just taken a bite of the beach. She blinked. Her eyes teared up. She reached to rub the sting away.

"Holly." Someone coughed.

Preston? She opened her eyes, but all she could see was a haze. Was she dreaming? Funny, she didn't remember going to bed. All she remembered was…Caleb with a shovel and the smell of gasoline.

Holly pushed her hands into the floor to sit up. Long's vacation rental really had been set on fire. But at least Preston had found her. And she was still alive.

The thick air choked her. Even her nostrils burned. She bent over as a coughing fit racked her chest.

"I'm getting you outside." Two strong arms scooped beneath her knees and arms. "Mrs. Long isn't here, is she?"

Holly shook her head as much as she could in the middle of a coughing fit. Was she still in danger? Not if Caleb had been caught. And he must have been if Preston had told the police what had happened and they'd let him go. The police would finally be on their side.

Preston stumbled toward the French doors at the rear of the home and yanked one open. Cool air rushed past them. Holly closed her eyes to fully enjoy a cleansing breath.

Boom. An invisible wall burst from within the house, propelling them off the deck and echoing across the canal.

Flames singed Holly's hair. Heat broiled her skin. The sand rushed up to catch her, and she rolled through it into the cool water. She half expected the lake to start sizzling at her touch. Instead, the waves soothed and cooled.

Footsteps pounded up the opposite side of the deck. A firefighter coming to extinguish the flames? A medic arriving to treat her burns?

Preston gripped her wrist and pulled her out deeper into the lake, then underneath the dock. She wrapped her arms around his neck and floated along. He could be her hero if he wanted. She was safe with him.

Her eyes adjusted to the dim light, and she searched Preston's face to meet his gaze. She'd been with him under a dock once before. Did he want another moment alone? She opened her mouth to tease him.

Footsteps thudded above just like they had during that game of hide-and-seek when she was sixteen. She smiled softly at the memory. Jake had never found them under the dock. It wasn't until Preston's funeral that she'd told her brother of her first kiss. But it wasn't Jake they were hiding from today. So who was it?

Holly glanced up through the cracks. Brand-new colorful hiking boots. No. She gripped Preston's shoulders. Why was Caleb still free? If the police had let Preston go, then they should have caught Caleb by now.

Preston raised his right wrist. Handcuffs dangled.

Her eyes bulged. Preston had escaped police custody?

Boards squeaked overhead. Water lapped her body. Her skin chilled. She clung tighter to Preston. Because if she made one noise, they would both be dead.

Caleb cocked his gun. He pointed the barrel up and down the planks above their heads as if listening for movement and trying to decide where to shoot first.

Sirens grew louder. Tires screeched.

Caleb sheathed the weapon inside his windbreaker. "I'm so glad you're here, Shaw," Holly's former fiancé called toward the arriving cops. His footsteps echoed in the space underneath the planks as he strode away.

She exhaled.

Shaw began his line of questioning. "Preston hijacked the helicopter. What happened?"

What was he talking about? Preston hijacked a helicopter?

"Holly started this fire to kill Commander Long's wife."

She had not. Caleb had attempted to burn her alive. Her blood boiled as if she were still in the house.

"I tried to stop her, Officer Shaw, but then Preston showed up in the helicopter and made the flames worse.

I had to shoot him down so the passengers would be safe, but he ducked out of the way, and I think I accidentally hit the pilot because Preston is the one who landed the thing."

Caleb might not have killed her, but he'd shot a pilot.

Her insides turned to ice.

"I don't think he's seriously injured, though I'll pay all his medical expenses. The man is a hero." Caleb's never-ending lies faded with his retreat.

Preston's muscles tensed under her touch.

Holly bit her lip. Was Caleb ever going to be stopped? She couldn't judge others for believing his lies when she'd fallen for his charm as hard as anyone. But it didn't help their situation.

"That's not good for us," she whispered.

"No, it's not." Preston's eyes roved over their under-water sanctuary as he thought. "He knows we're here. He's trying to distract the emergency workers so he can come back here alone and finish what he started."

Holly gripped his shoulders tighter. Would their night-mare ever end? "What do we do?"

Preston pulled her deeper. "We're going to swim under-water to the next dock before Caleb comes back. And we'll keep going like that until we get far enough away to escape him."

Holly nodded. She'd been trying to help by tracking down Mrs. Long, but she'd almost gotten herself killed again, and now both of them were in danger.

She held her breath and submerged herself in the cool water. Preston dived down beside her, pulling her after him when her shoulder threatened to give out. Together, they broke surface under a boat slip owned by the neigh-bors.

She sucked oxygen before repeating the swim to an-other dock around the curve of the peninsula, then across the canal to the docks lining the houses on a different street. They could climb out here without fear of getting caught.

Holly clung to Preston to help slow the shivering. She was too tired to move. And she was too tired to pretend she didn't want to stay in his arms forever.

His lips dropped to her temple, like a stone skipping across a lake and making ripples with each touch. He must have felt the same way she did. All she had to do was lift her chin to kiss him back. Her toes curled as his nose dropped down to nuzzle her. He was even closer now. Her heart ticked away each excruciating second she waited for his lips to touch hers. Just like it had when they were sixteen.

His mouth covered hers, warming her from the inside. Her hand lifted to cup his face, the rough stubble along his jaw reminding her things had changed since they'd first kissed under a dock.

No, he wasn't a kid anymore, but being with him brought back the sincerity and innocence of their youth. Would they ever get the chance for a fresh start?

Oh. The newspaper article. She jumped, breaking their connection. Her chest heaved and not just from the way Preston had kissed her breathless. While escaping a burning building, swimming to safety, then experiencing the most romantic moment of her life, she'd forgotten to tell him about the connection with Sergeant Matthew Hayes.

"I have something to tell you."

He paused a moment before dragging his gaze up from her lips. "You don't want me to kiss you anymore?"

"No."

His eyebrows arched toward his hairline.

She laughed at her mistake. "I mean, yes. I do." Her face burned. When was the last time she'd blushed? He made her feel like a teenager all over again. "But there's something that's going to make you want to kiss me even more."

"I can't imagine."

Oh, the distractions. She better spit it out while she could. "I looked up that newspaper article again, and I found a second article in the same paper mentioning Sergeant Hayes." She explained the connection. "Preston, he's probably—"

"—the mechanic Commander Long hired," Preston finished for her. "I can't believe I never suspected as much."

She clasped his hand to remind them they were stronger as a team. "You didn't know Long was involved."

Preston's gaze roamed the planks above them. He shook his head. "Unfortunately, Long can't be questioned. And I'm sure Caleb will find a way to pin the sergeant's death on me, as well."

"But it wasn't you." Now that they knew the truth and she had found the article, they were one step closer to proving Preston innocent. He couldn't give up now.

Would one article in the newspaper be enough to give a jury reasonable doubt and keep them from convicting him? Not likely.

He drew Holly to his side. She'd tried, but there were no more options for evidence. Long and Lee were both dead. Hank was shot. And Denise was apparently on the run.

Holly was going to have her work cut out for her in defending him. But he'd rather go to prison than let the list of deaths and injuries grow any longer.

Preston's chest constricted around his heart as if trying to protect it from the ache of loneliness he'd only recently allowed himself to feel. He buried his face in Holly's hair. The smoky smell reminded him of what she'd barely survived. "We have to turn ourselves in."

She bit her lip. "You think the police believe Caleb's lies?"

Preston shrugged in defeat. "They said they'd investigate, but for now, he's still on the loose. Which means you'd be safest in a jail cell."

"He confessed to me on the boat. I wish I'd had my phone so that I could have recorded him." Her head snapped back up. "Hey, what if we let him think he'd caught us?"

Preston tilted his head to get out any remaining water from his ear because he couldn't have heard her right. "You didn't just say you wanted to let Caleb think he caught us again, did you?"

"Yes, I did. Only, this time, we can record him when he confesses everything."

"No way." Preston's heart lurched at the thought. He'd go to jail for life before he put her in jeopardy again. "Caleb used you as bait to get to me because he didn't care what happened to you. That's not something I would ever do."

"Preston," she whispered, leaning close and looking up into his eyes in a way that made him want to rush into a burning building for her all over again. "I tried living without you once, and I don't want to do it again."

"But at least you'll live." Was it too late to run away together and make fake identities for themselves? If only he'd admitted his feelings for her the day before. He couldn't do it now. Not when the best thing for her would be to move on without him.

She pulled away and wiped at tears. "Stop it. Stop saying goodbye."

He could go after her. He could kiss her until her anger subsided. But what good would that do? He'd do what had to be done. What he'd always done. Lock up his emotions because she'd be better off without him. "I want the best for you, Holly. I'm not going to let you get hurt."

Holly bit her lip. "You don't have to do this alone, Preston. We can work together. We can overcome this together." Her voice cracked. "Haven't we made a pretty good team so far?"

She'd been the best teammate ever. She'd even been willing to jump off a cliff with a bullet wound when he'd told her to. And then she'd ended up in the middle of a cabin in flames. "Yes. But nothing we've tried has worked. You've been shot." He motioned in the direction they'd come from. "Hank's been shot." He crossed his arms to keep from wrapping them around her again. "You almost got burned alive just now."

She floated back his way. "You saved me. You're my hero."

He was no hero. But that wasn't the point. "Holly, if I'd turned myself in at the police station like I'd planned to, this never would have happened. I can't take the risk of anything else happening to you."

She stopped moving toward him. Though the distance between them was more than just physical.

"Are you giving up on God again?" she asked.

"No. He's given up on me." Preston had prayed, and it hadn't been enough. Yes, her find in the newspaper was huge, but it didn't stop bullets. It didn't put out flames.

"I believe God is always here for us," she whispered.

He pressed his lips together. Faith was his weakness. But she had weaknesses, too. "Well, then, Holly. God's going to have to be enough for you."

"What…" Her eyes stilled in fear. "What do you mean?"

"I mean you're more likely to be set free by a jury than I am. And then either God can be enough for you or you can find yourself another man to marry."

She sucked in her breath, and he almost wished he could take back his words. Almost. Except for the fact that her anger would keep her away from him, and he wouldn't be as tempted to hold her again or succumb to her dangerous plans for finding evidence against Caleb.

She lifted her chin to disguise its trembling. "I can't believe you said that."

That familiar prick of guilt threatened to make him apologize. Maybe he really was the bad guy she'd accused him of acting like before. But he had to be if he was going to keep her safe from the danger that followed him. "Time will tell if I'm right or not. Now let's go see if the owners of this house will let us call Officer Shaw from their phone."

He deserved to be locked up for the way he'd just treated an innocent woman. He submerged himself underwater to lead her out into the open. Plus, if he was underwater, he wouldn't have to see the hurt in her expression. Too bad he had to face her when he came back up. Or he could focus on other things.

Smoke filled the air around the dock, and boaters gawked at the sight of emergency workers surrounding the smoldering home behind them. Preston wiped his face and double-checked for a sign of Caleb. He'd been worried the gunman would suspect their escape route and make his way from dock to dock until he located them. But perhaps the man had searched the docks in the opposite direction. At least Caleb didn't have his car or boat to chase them this time. And Shaw had also said the police would be keeping an eye on him.

Preston let Holly trail behind as he trudged up onto the shore into someone's backyard and wrung out his shirt. An older woman stood on the deck, staring down at him as he emerged from the water. Probably not a sight she saw every day.

"Excuse me," he started.

The woman's eyes focused on the handcuffs hanging from his wrist. She backed up.

Holly stepped in front of him, taking the lead. She was really going to rescue him after the way he'd just treated her? "Ma'am, as you can see, this man escaped from police custody recently. I need to use your phone to call the authorities and turn him in."

Some rescue. But she spoke the truth.

The woman already had a phone in her hand. She looked back past her house toward the street. "I…I called security when I heard your voices under the dock. They're on their way."

Private security for the property owners association? Also known as rent-a-cops? Preston would take what he could get.

But he couldn't keep the sarcasm out of his voice. "Nice, Holly."

She squinted in his direction. "You're the one so intent on going to prison." At least she wasn't fighting him anymore. She addressed the woman on the deck. "Thank you, ma'am."

Preston crossed his arms as they rounded the house and stood on the sidewalk, awaiting the white SUV with green lettering rolling down the street. Should he keep up his nonchalance, or should he let his walls crumble?

"Hey," he said. Where the opening would lead, he didn't know.

She peeked up.

His heart pulled against the restraints he'd used to hold it back.

She was alive. And she was by his side. That was pretty

amazing after what they'd been through. He couldn't end it like this.

The security vehicle braked in front of them.

Preston took a deep breath and reached for her hand. He knew how much she hated being by herself. He couldn't let her feel alone while he was right there next to her.

But the warmth of her touch traveled to his core. He hadn't steeled his feelings well enough.

She bit her lip. She blinked a couple times before looking up. And he knew in that moment that he loved her. Loved everything about her. Loved her passion. Loved her tenacity. Loved her faith.

No matter what their future brought, he was going to fight for her. And he was going to win. He hated being the bad guy. Especially to the one person who believed him innocent.

Two doors clicked open. Two security guards? Preston looked up to explain his situation to the men on duty. He had to make sure they took it easy on Holly.

Caleb climbed out of the passenger seat. "That's her. That's my fiancée. Let her go, Preston."

Preston jolted. How was this possible? Caleb had turned more good guys against him. They'd have to run again.

SEVENTEEN

Holly's body froze. She hadn't wanted Preston to turn himself in to the police, but she didn't want to have to keep running, either. She'd just wanted to get one step ahead of the creep who'd tried to kill her, though Caleb must have somehow managed to convince the local security guard to help him find her, claiming they were still engaged. The man in uniform would be on her side once he heard the whole story, but she couldn't stick around to explain it all knowing her former fiancé had a gun.

Caleb lunged.

Preston tugged her out of reach, setting her body in motion. He might not be part of her future, but he was going to make sure she survived the present.

She turned and sprinted. Her surroundings blurred together. Her thoughts tried to do the same.

Would Caleb fire his gun? Would he take the patrol car and chase them down? There was only one road out of there.

"Stop," the security guard shouted.

If only they could.

Preston's arms and legs pumped along beside her. Where were they going? What were they doing?

An engine revved behind them.

Her breath spasmed. Her heart pounded. To get to police, they'd have to make it to the end of the road, turn left and backtrack down White Sands Drive. There were no shortcuts…unless they swam across the canal again.

The engine revved louder until it drowned out her own pulse and buzzed through her body. If they didn't get off the road, they would be caught.

She chanced a glance over her shoulder. Her stomach flipped at the sight of Caleb behind the wheel.

The car was close enough that its heat warmed her calves. Preston's body careened into hers, knocking her into the grass. The vehicle charged by. They rolled together, the pain of impact barely registering through the realization they'd almost been run over.

There was no stopping Caleb. Preston had been right about going to police. They needed to get back to the water and swim for it. "To the water?"

"Yeah."

She pushed to a squat and took off between two houses like a sprinter at the sound of a starter pistol. Her feet pounded grass. She ducked under a tree. Grazed past a bush. Tires screeched as Caleb turned his stolen vehicle around, but he couldn't follow her into the water with a car. "We can make it."

No response.

"Preston?" She craned her neck around without slowing down.

Her heart thudded to a stop. Her feet skidded through the grass into the dirt to slow her momentum. She was alone.

"Preston?" she yelled this time.

Had he been hurt? Caught? She doubled back.

There he was. Running down the street in the direction they'd come from as fast as she'd run between the houses.

He must be heading toward the dock they'd hid under. It would be a shorter swim to the house on White Sands that way, but it would take longer to get to the water and away from Caleb.

Preston's head swiveled. He caught sight of her and tripped over his own feet coming to a halt. He hadn't realized she'd run a different direction, either. His brows rose in surprise. Then his gaze bounced behind her and his eyes grew wider.

A car engine revved. Did she keep going between houses to get away, leaving Preston to continue on his path? Or would they try to reunite before Caleb reached them?

Two are better than one. She would believe that even when he didn't. She would have been hit earlier if he hadn't pushed her out of the way. She might not survive without him now. She charged forward. Through people's lawns this time so Caleb wouldn't be able to run her down.

Preston ran, as well. Toward her and ultimately toward Caleb. Behind Preston, a stunned security guard grappled with a walkie-talkie. A lot of help he was.

In the distance, a police boat chugged through the water toward their side of the canal. Maybe the woman who'd called security had also called the police. Or maybe the car chase was making such a commotion that Shaw had noticed from the other side of the channel. They'd be saved.

Preston couldn't see what she saw. He didn't know police were on the way. He still raced toward her, intensity flashing in his eyes as if he had to rescue her.

She hadn't reached him yet, but when she did, he'd need to turn around so they could get help. Then they'd be able to breathe easy again while the lawmen did the chasing.

Preston pointed. Yelled her name.

The white SUV shot beside her. Her reflexes pushed

her feet to race faster. Blood roared in her ears. Was she still going to get run over?

The vehicle swerved into the grass in front of her.

Her hands flew up to protect her body. She flexed her thighs and pressed her heels into the ground to slow her speed, but she couldn't stop. The car didn't hit her. She hit it. Bounced off. Caught herself before tumbling to the ground, but it took a moment to right her senses. To focus clearly on her surroundings. To let the world stop spinning.

The passenger-side door clicked open. She braced to scramble back.

An arm shot through the opening. A hand grabbed her wrist and yanked.

She tumbled forward onto the passenger's seat. Screamed. Pushed to her knees. Clawed at the man who held her.

"Holly!" Preston yelled again. But he was too far away.

She had to fight Caleb off herself. Before it was too late.

But the car was already moving. Crashing through a bush to face the other direction. The outlet. Away from the police boat. Away from the security guard. Away from Preston.

Holly yanked and twisted to throw herself out of the moving vehicle. Caleb's grip slipped from her skin. She could do this.

The car swerved. The door slammed in her face.

The barrel of a gun poked into her back. Her breath caught.

"If you grab the handle, I will shoot you right now."

Could she move fast enough to get away? She hadn't been fast enough to avoid the bullet that had hit her arm. The abrasion throbbed, reminding her how fragile life was.

But if she obeyed Caleb, would he really let her live? He'd killed the two people who were working with him, so what chance did she have?

The man slapped the wheel with one hand to turn the

corner. Preston's running form disappeared behind vacation homes. At least he was alive. At least Caleb hadn't gotten him. And now he could go to the police. Caleb would be stopped whether he killed her or not.

Her toes curled at the very real possibility he'd shoot her first. Her best chance for survival could be to play along.

"Pick up the radio."

Caleb wanted to listen to music? That was better than talking to him. She eased away from the gun digging into her spine so she could face forward. But she refused to look at him as she reached a trembling hand toward the dial.

He knocked the gun against her knuckles.

She pulled her hand back and massaged the sting. What was that for?

"No, the two-way radio."

Her heart shimmied. He was going to let her talk to someone? She hesitantly wrapped her fingers around the transmitter, lest he pistol whip her again.

"The security guard's name is Brett. Call Brett."

She eyed Caleb. Was he losing it? Why did the bad guy want her to call security?

"Do it."

She lifted the receiver to her mouth and pressed the button. "Brett?" Her voice wavered. Should she scream for help? Let whoever was listening know that rather than turning right to exit the Keys, Caleb was turning left into the heart of the resort?

Caleb motioned with the gun for her to speak further.

"Is Brett there?"

Static crackled. "This is Brett Reynolds. Who am I speaking with?"

Holly squeezed the transmitter like a lifeline. Words

leaped out of her mouth. "This is Holly Fontaine, and I'm—"

The gun smacked the side of her face.

Her head bounced into the back of the seat. She flinched in case there was another blow coming. When Caleb didn't strike a second time, she pressed a cool palm to her burning cheek.

"Have him call my cell. Give him the number."

Holly blinked away tears. She lowered her head to make sure Caleb didn't see her cry. She hated the fact she knew Caleb's number by heart because she used to call him all the time. He'd always been a good listener. Now she knew why. She gave Brett the phone number.

The cellular device on the center console vibrated.

Holly jumped. Now what?

Caleb nodded toward her. "Answer it and put it on speaker."

Police could trace the call, right? And there was probably even a GPS tracker in the vehicle. She was going to be rescued. She just had to keep Caleb pacified.

She lifted the phone and pressed the appropriate buttons on the screen.

Caleb pulled through rows of condos into the actual resort parking lot. He hadn't gone very far. Why were they stopping?

"Brett." Caleb took over. "This is what's going to happen."

Holly eyed the man. How could he be acting like he had everything under control when he should have been waving the white flag? He was crazy. Should she try to get away while he was distracted with the conversation? She shifted her gaze to the windshield.

She needed people around as witnesses. People who could use their own cell phones to call for help. People to usher her into their condos and lock the door until help arrived. But would she just be putting them in danger?

Caleb rolled to a stop between two pickups. He shifted into Park with his free hand while leveling the gun back on her as if daring her to try to escape. "Brett, you're going to report your vehicle stolen to the police arriving on the scene. You're going to tell them Preston and Holly took it and that it had my phone in it."

What? She may have God on her side, but she needed the police, too.

"If you don't tell police what I want you to, I'm going to kill both Preston and Holly, then come after you."

No. No more death. Holly choked back a sob. Caleb couldn't get away with this, could he? Though why not? She'd said her name over the two-way radio. She'd given Brett the number of the phone the police would be told was in Preston and Holly's possession. And the police arriving on the scene would have only seen the vehicle take off. But what about Preston still being there?

"Now give the phone to Preston."

Her pulse thrummed against her throat, in her thumbs and behind her knees.

Muffled noises rang over the speaker as the security officer complied.

"Caleb, you liar," Preston shouted. Just the sound of his voice gave Holly strength. "I'm not taking the fall for your crimes. I'm going to the police, and if you so much as touch Holly, I will—"

Caleb glared at Holly, the heat of his gaze singeing her soul. "You go to the police, and she's dead."

Silence. "How do I know you haven't already killed her?"

Caleb dug the gun into her side until she winced. "Say hi, Holly."

Holly narrowed her eyes. The man was still using her

as bait. If she went along with it, he'd kill them both. But if she didn't say anything, Caleb could shoot her right there. Preston would hear the gunshot. He'd have to mourn her the way she'd once mourned him. But at least Caleb would get caught, and he couldn't hurt anyone else.

She leaned forward to make sure her words came through clearly. "We're parked at the resort. Caleb didn't leave the Tahoe Keys. He's—"

The gun slammed down into her thigh. Pain shot both up and down her leg, mangling the sensation of individual muscles. The air in her lungs grunted away. She gripped the seat with her fingernails and writhed to suck in another breath.

"Make no mistake, Preston. If you want to see her alive, you will do exactly as I say. First, you will get out of sight so the police believe Brett's story. Second, you will meet me in the center of Fanny Bridge at midnight tonight. Alone."

Preston squeezed the phone tighter. He felt angry enough to crush the thing. But he'd be better off using the energy to catch Caleb. Holly had said they were at the resort. He took off down the road, the phone still to his ear.

"Why would I meet you alone?" he challenged. There was no way Preston wouldn't show, but if he could keep Caleb talking, the man might not have the time to get away before Preston caught up to him. "So you could kill us both?"

"Wait," the security guard yelled from behind him, not sounding as confident as he had before. Of course, he'd just had his life threatened.

The best way for Preston to help the man would be to get Caleb behind bars so the killer couldn't make good on his threat. As to whether the security guard told police the truth or not, it didn't really matter. Preston was the only one who knew where Caleb was and what Caleb wanted.

Heavy breathing rang through the phone as if Caleb was physically exerting himself while he spoke. Preston's tactics to stall the kidnapping must not have been effective.

"You'll come because you think you can save Holly," Caleb finally responded. "That's what you do."

Preston had been successful so far. And nothing would keep him from believing he could save her again. Maybe he had more hope than he'd want to admit. But was it hope in God or hope in himself? In his own abilities?

Preston reached the end of the road, but he didn't turn the way Caleb had. He'd take the shortcut through the front lawns to backyards, to the tennis courts that separated homes from the condos.

Preston held the phone away from his mouth as he panted. He didn't want Caleb to know he was coming for him. He took a deep breath to respond evenly, "I *am* going to save Holly."

Caleb chuckled.

Preston continued past the condos into the parking lot, which was flanked on three sides with the actual resort. Where was Caleb?

"Even if it costs you your life?" Caleb asked.

No sight of the kidnapper. Preston's heart thudded in his ears. Holly had said they had parked here. Had Caleb backed out once he knew Preston was aware of his location? Preston circled the parking lot to be sure.

What had Caleb asked? If he would give his life for Holly? What a stupid question. That was why Preston had played dead in the first place. Of all people, Caleb knew he would give his life for hers. "You know I would."

There. The white security vehicle. Empty.

Preston spun in a circle, the area now overwhelmingly large. Where had Caleb gone? Inside one of the buildings? No. Not if he was trying to get away.

Preston sprinted down the sidewalk toward the marina. Was he heading in the right direction or wasting precious time? For all he knew, Caleb could be watching through a window and laughing inside.

"I'm counting on it," Caleb responded, voice menacing. In the background, a boat engine revved. The same sound that came from a dock at the other end of the pier.

Preston pivoted and pushed off through the soles of his shoes. He was close. Just not close enough. In the distance a red ski boat with a wakeboard tower shot toward the channel leading out of the marina.

Preston charged down the pathway in pursuit but slid to a stop at the edge of the dock. They were too far away for him to catch up without a boat of his own. And there were no nearby boaters who could give him a lift.

He stared helplessly after Holly. Why hadn't she jumped overboard? Why had she just sat there? That wasn't like her. Unless she was hurt. His heart jammed into his throat as he watched her double over and hug one knee.

"See you at midnight, Preston." Caleb tossed the phone into his wake. He'd won again.

EIGHTEEN

Holly shifted on the boat to ease the throbbing pressure in her thigh. Part of her wanted to know what Preston had been doing in the hours since Caleb had kidnapped her and taken off in the stolen boat to hide out in an area of the lake out of sight from the freeway called Hidden Beach. Had he gone to the police? Had they been formulating a plan to rescue her? Were they aware of her location and closing in?

But then her questions would dissolve as waves of pain overtook her emotions. She hated the whimpering sound coming from her lips. She hated that Caleb hadn't even had to tie her up to keep her in place, and the one time she'd tried to escape, she'd ended up in a heap at the bottom of the boat without him even touching her. She hated that the man she'd been planning to pledge her life to that very day now reveled in her misery.

"It's almost over, sweetheart."

She opened her eyes to glare through the darkness. If he took one step closer, she'd slap that smile off his face.

He moved to the steering wheel and turned the ignition, then putted toward the anchor while simultaneously pressing the button to pull it up.

The boat vibrated. She gritted her teeth. Her pain was

barely tolerable when she kept her leg in place, but if Caleb took the ski boat back on the open water, she'd be bouncing all over again. She leaned forward and wrapped fingers around her leg to hold it as still as possible.

Why were they leaving Hidden Beach? Wouldn't Caleb want to keep the boat hidden? Not to mention he needed to get to dry land if he was going to meet Preston on the bridge.

Caleb locked the anchor into storage, jostling the boat. She stiffened at the impact. If just that small movement ignited her thigh, how was she ever going to make it over open water?

She moaned. "Are you going to leave me here?"

Caleb returned to the helm. "I need you. Why do you think you're still alive?"

She shook her head to clear her thoughts. She didn't know anything anymore.

"I'm fishing for Preston, and you're the bait."

That was all she'd ever been to him. No wonder she felt as helpless as a worm on a hook.

The boat slid quietly forward through the night. Caleb didn't even use a light. She should relax knowing she wasn't up for a wild ride, but the pain of a wild ride would have been preferable if he made enough noise and movement to get caught.

She'd been praying nonstop from the moment she'd seen Caleb with the security guard, but it had brought her no peace. Maybe God had orchestrated some kind of rescue without her knowledge, but maybe not. Maybe she was going to die alone.

Being alone was to her what claustrophobia was to other people. She'd so much rather be confined in a tight place with other people than surrounded with emptiness all by herself.

Had Preston been right about her? That was what had hurt the most about his statement earlier. She always wanted someone to rescue her.

She couldn't even feel God's presence. The Bible said she was never alone, but the night told her otherwise. There was no one out there who knew where she was. The world was so big. She was so small. She didn't matter.

She clutched her hands to her sides and curled into herself to block out the expanse of stars and volume of her breath. She'd talk to Caleb. Because even a bad guy was better than nobody. Or was that the belief that had gotten her into this situation in the first place? Too late to change that now.

"What are you going to do with me when you go to meet Preston? I can't walk."

Then she'd really be all alone.

"You don't have to walk."

She looked up. Was he going to take her back to his car? Make Preston chase them up into the mountains, where he could kill them both without any witnesses around? Surely the drive would give them time to overpower him and—

"We're going to float right under the bridge." He focused forward on the lights in the distance. Tahoe City.

If they floated under the bridge, Preston would see her and leap to save her. Then Caleb would have them both on his boat. He could shoot them and throw them overboard. But if that was his plan… "Why didn't you just let him leap on board earlier? You could have taken care of us then."

"Police were there. I needed to get away. And I needed to make sure the authorities bought the story about you and Preston taking off in the security vehicle." Caleb shrugged. "According to the police radio I tapped into, you two are currently wanted criminals."

Panic crawled up her spine, paralyzing her body. *Do something, Lord.*

The town grew larger. A boat flashed past, its light almost blinding. Her eyes readjusted. The shadow of a bridge appeared in the horizon. Was that a man standing in the center?

Caleb looked at his watch. "Right on time."

No. How could God let this happen? Maybe Preston was right. Maybe God didn't really answer prayers.

Or maybe she'd been praying the wrong thing. Maybe God had a plan, and He was waiting for her to follow it. *Tell me what to do, Lord.*

Preston had risked his life to save her. Was she willing to do the same for him? She would if she loved him.

Peace flooded her soul. Because love wasn't about having someone there for her. It was about being willing to be there for someone else. The way Jesus was there for her.

She wasn't alone. She was never alone.

The bridge grew closer as the boat sliced through the water, into the mouth of Truckee River. There was no question Preston would jump on board to save her. But what could she do to save him?

Scream for help? Grab the radio? Try to get Caleb's gun?

Preston's form climbed atop the bridge railing. He crouched, ready to spring. She had to act before he could. What could she do to guarantee Caleb would stop the boat before Preston boarded?

Only one thing.

She gripped smooth fiberglass, took a deep breath and pushed with her good foot to propel herself overboard.

The cold water embraced her, threatened to smother her. Its icy sting seeped into her pores and warred for attention with the ache in her leg. She kicked her right foot and arched toward the surface. And she'd thought swimming with a gunshot wound had been challenging.

Her mouth broke the surface. She gasped for breath and leaned back to float, blinking to find Preston's form through the blur of water droplets.

A wave of water rolled over her face, blocking him from view. The lake splashed and gurgled behind her. Water washed into her lungs. She coughed against the onslaught.

Something slick slid around her neck. A hand. Squeezing. Pulling her back under. Caleb must have jumped in after her.

She shot an elbow his direction, but the lake slowed its progress, lessened its impact.

Water shot up her nose, tingling in her sinuses. She blew out to keep from inhaling any more. But she'd have to get another breath soon.

Would Preston reach her in time to save her? Wait. That wasn't what she wanted. She wanted him to stay far away from Caleb. But he wouldn't as long as he thought she needed help.

Caleb's fingers threaded through her hair and held her head facedown while keeping her body at a distance so she couldn't reach him to fight. She clawed and kicked, the movement creating a greater need for air.

So she stopped. She relaxed. Let her arms and legs float to the surface. Caleb wouldn't keep trying to drown her if he thought she was already dead.

Her lungs burned. The lake water stung. Her thigh throbbed. But she didn't move.

Hair slithered silently around her. And despite the pain, she knew she would survive. Because as Preston had once said, it wasn't the *how* that mattered. If the *why* was important enough, the *how* just happened.

Her why was pretty important. She needed to play dead to save someone else's life.

* * *

Preston squinted as the red ski boat rocked into the light. Where was Caleb? Where was Holly? The boat hadn't steered itself up Truckee River.

The boat floated forward, revealing two figures in the water behind it. What was Caleb up to? Was he trying to distract Preston with the boat so he could sneak around behind him on the bridge? But how was he going to do that with Holly as his captive? Especially if Holly was injured.

The figures thrashed. His muscles flexed in reaction. Had Holly jumped overboard? He didn't know. He just knew he needed to be there for her the way he'd ached to be all day. He'd been planning to jump into the boat to rescue her. Maybe he still could.

It drifted toward him. He'd jump in and turn it around to reach Holly much faster than he could swim to her.

He sprung forward into midair. Gravity pulled. He softened his knees to brace for impact.

His feet slammed into fiberglass. The jolt traveled up his spine, jarring his senses, but he stayed standing. Now where was Holly?

No more splashing. What did that mean? Had she gotten free? He cranked the steering wheel to spin the boat around while jabbing at the dashboard until a blue light flicked on underwater.

One silhouette swam toward him. But it was the silhouette of a man. Where was Holly?

Preston gunned the engine to reach the spot where he'd seen her last. He turned off the gas to float, frantically scanning the water for her body. Had she sunk? Did he need to dive in?

Dread clawed at his heart. But he refused to let it in. He'd fought too hard. Given up too much. He could find her. He could do this. Because he certainly couldn't go on without her. Not now that he'd let himself love.

There. Floating behind some rocks near the shore. That had to be her hair. But why was she floating? Facedown? No...

He grabbed the wheel again. Lessons in CPR flashed through his consciousness. He'd breathe for her. He'd pump her heart for her. He'd keep her alive until an ambulance came. He had to.

Metal clattered behind him. Rubber squeaked. Preston shot a glance over his shoulder to find Caleb back on board.

Oh no. He didn't have time to fight for his own life. He had to fight for Holly's. He thrust the boat forward to knock the man off his feet.

Caleb grabbed on to the railing in time to keep from falling. He lunged. Swung a fist.

Preston ducked. He'd avoided the blow but hit his head on the dash. The crack zapped pain through his temple to his skull. He gritted his teeth and opened his eyes to retaliate. But he didn't have to. Because there, sitting in front of him, was Caleb's gun.

He grasped for the cold metal, slid his fingers around the grip and pivoted to level the barrel at Caleb.

Caleb held up both hands.

A beam of light on the riverbank shone down upon him. Blue and red lights flashed from a police boat. The whipping sound of a helicopter signaled the arrival of scuba divers, who dropped into the water around them.

"Stop. STPD," a voice spoke over a bullhorn.

Preston raised one hand to surrender and the other one to shade the light from his eyes to find Holly. She was nowhere to be seen. Must have floated around the rock. Had help gotten there in time?

Caleb pointed toward the rock. "Preston killed Holly," he lied. "I swam out to this boat he stole to try to save her, but then he pulled a gun on me."

Preston stared at the chaos. He stared at the man who'd ruined his life. He stared at the spot he'd last seen Holly. Surely, if she'd survived, she would have crawled up onto the rock to see what was going on. Or she'd be yelling the truth at the top of her lungs.

Numbness crept over his skin and seeped inside. The kind of numbness that froze his heart like liquid nitrogen so that, when reality crashed in, it would shatter like glass.

What had he done? He'd put his hope in himself rather than God. And he hadn't been enough.

NINETEEN

Preston stared at his handcuffs in the interrogation room. Soon his existence would be all over the news. His parents would probably show up at the police station. They'd be elated at his return until they realized he was likely going to be accused of murder. He'd be blamed for the death of Commander Long, not to mention his team in the helicopter. He'd be the most hated man in America. But that wasn't the worst thing that could happen to him.

The worst thing that could happen was for him to be set free knowing Holly died in his place.

He extended his arms forward and dropped his head to the hard, metal table. If only he hadn't said such hurtful things to her under the dock. If only he hadn't tried to be the Lone Ranger again. He'd felt bad about pushing her away like that, which was why he hadn't been focused on the security vehicle when it showed up in the keys. Which was why he'd been distracted enough to let her get kidnapped.

But even if Caleb would have gotten to her anyway, Preston could have at least told her he loved her. Instead of insinuating that she was shallow enough to replace him the moment he went to jail.

She wasn't like that. She was the opposite. She'd fought

for him so hard that she'd lost her life. While he'd self-ishly turned on God for not avenging him of his enemies on his own personal timeline.

He'd wasted the time he had with Holly because he'd convinced himself he was doing the right thing by re-fusing to connect. Had he known their couple of days to-gether were going to be all she'd have left on Earth, he would have savored every moment. And he would have prayed more.

It was too late for a relationship with Holly, but it wasn't too late for a relationship with the Lord. "Oh, God." He spoke aloud, uncaring if his words were recorded. He had nothing to hide anymore. In fact, he hoped the cops were listening. He hoped other people could learn from his mistakes.

"I'm so sorry." Did the CID investigators watching through the two-way glass assume he was confessing? Well, he was. "I'm sorry Holly died so I could live." But Holly wasn't the only one who'd died for him. Jesus had also died so he could live. Though he'd never gotten it be-fore. He'd squandered the gift. "I'm so sorry I thought I could do it on my own. I'm so sorry I didn't put my hope in You."

His voice broke. He choked back a sob.

He would choose to believe all things worked together for good now. But that didn't stop the overwhelming hurt of the moment. The kind of hurt he'd put all his loved ones through. The kind of pain God must have felt when let-ting His son die on the cross.

Preston didn't know how others handled the grief, but he'd learned he couldn't do things on his own. He had to put his hope in the Lord.

"Please help me, God."

The door clicked open. Shoes slapped cement. Time to answer questions.

Preston took a deep breath through his constricted throat. Drained of energy, his body wanted to sink deeper into the table, but he'd caused the government enough trouble for one day. He'd rise and face his problems, knowing God was still on his side. He couldn't bring back Holly, but he could fight for justice for her.

He rolled up, the ache in his spine rising one vertebrae at a time until it settled as tension in his shoulders. He lifted his chin to defend himself. "I didn't kill Holly. I—"

The gray gaze caressed him at the same time it pierced his soul. "I know," she said.

His breath rushed out as if someone had punched him in the gut. How could it be? How could Holly be standing in front of him on crutches? He'd seen her float away, facedown.

"You—" He stood. He didn't need to piece it together as much as he needed to hold her.

She tried to wobble his way, but he was faster. He looped his handcuffs over her head and behind her neck, laughing at the situation. So what if he went to prison for life? He'd learned how to love. And that was what really mattered.

She shifted her weight to one foot and grasped both crutches in the opposite hand to wrap a free arm behind his back. Her chin lifted until they were face-to-face. Her heart beat against his chest.

She was so warm. So soft. So alive.

"I thought you drowned."

She bit her lip. Her eyes searched his. "I played dead."

There were no words. He shook his head in wonder. Studied each inch of her face to memorize her features. He had to make the most of every moment with her. It was a gift. God had given them a second chance. Or was it a third chance? He wouldn't squander this one.

The vise around his heart unclamped. He could breathe again. "Promise me you'll never do that again."

Her eyes glossed over as if in pain.

Her leg? Or her memory of him playing dead first? He had no way to comfort her but to tilt his forehead against hers. "I'm just glad you're okay."

The corners of her mouth curved up. That was better. He never wanted to hurt her again.

Preston focused on her smile. Her lips. He still had some making up to do.

The door swooshed open. He wanted to ignore the interruption. To deepen their connection. But he *was* in police custody.

Officer Shaw cleared his throat.

Preston looked up. Smiled at the old guy. There was nothing the law could do to dampen his mood.

"Tyler, please have a seat."

Preston looked back down at Holly as he raised his arms over her head to end their embrace. She wobbled backward. He lowered himself to the chair, handcuffs on the table once again. Though he wanted to whoop and holler and jump around.

"Mr. Tyler, it's been a long couple of days, so I want to make this quick and get home to my wife."

Preston nodded. He could relate to the sentiment. Even if he had no wife and home to return to. Yet.

"We got a phone call about a boat without lights on and tracked it down to the bridge. We rescued Holly and found you and Caleb fighting."

Preston slid his gaze her direction and relaxed in contentment. Even when he'd doubted God's love and run from faith, God had never given up on him.

"The problem is that the story you're telling us is the same thing Caleb is telling us. You both claim the other hid the sabotage of Operation Desert Storm and has been killing people to cover it up. So we have you both in custody. Neither Denise Amador nor the security guard is willing to testify against him. They're afraid."

A wrinkle appeared between Holly's eyebrows. She would know more about testimonies than he did. But if she represented him in court, she could prove him innocent. She'd seemed pretty sure of herself when she'd found that newspaper article.

"Right now, it's your word against Caleb's. We have no evidence. Unless Holly testifies."

Preston glanced back at Shaw. Why did he seem so serious? So Holly would be a witness instead of his lawyer. That was still okay, wasn't it?

"I allowed Holly to come in here to say goodbye because she's agreed to be a witness, and for her own safety against Caleb hiring another hit man, we are going to have to put her in the Witness Security Program."

Preston leaped to his feet. They had to be kidding. He'd just gotten her back. "What? For how long? She's been in enough danger, and—"

Holly reached for his arm. The soft touch of her fingers brought little comfort. Because if she went into WitSec she wouldn't see her again for a long time. That was *if* he ever saw her again. He raised his hands to his hair and gripped the roots in frustration.

"It's okay, Preston," she consoled him. "This is the only way to free you."

Her goal. But not his. Not anymore. What could he do?

Nothing. He could do nothing. He'd tried to save her and failed. Only a moment ago he'd been promising to put all his hope in God, and already he'd forgotten. Had he learned nothing? *Oh, God, save Holly.*

If only he'd prayed this prayer earlier instead of praying for God to avenge his enemies. Wait. That was it. His mind rewound to his desperate plea outside the cave. He'd been comparing himself to David at the time. And he still should.

When David knew King Saul wanted him dead, Jonathan had trouble believing his dad would be so evil. So David told Jonathan to tell Saul that David was still alive and see how he reacted. Saul's anger revealed his true intentions.

They could do this to Caleb. On camera. The evidence would be hard for Caleb to explain away in court.

Preston lowered his hands. He studied Holly. The woman was willing to give up her life for him, but now she wouldn't have to.

"Does Caleb think Holly's dead?"

Holly's eyes widened. She glanced at Shaw for the response.

The officer shrugged. "Well, yes. We want to let him think she's dead until his trial gets to discovery and we have to reveal her as a witness. By then, she will be safely hidden, and he will have less time to try to track her down."

Preston sat up straight. Shaw's plan was a good one for the case, but not good for Holly. She wasn't dead. She had a life to live. "What if Holly reveals herself to Caleb the way she just did to me? You're going to get a whole different reaction."

Shaw crossed his arms. "That's not normal procedure."

Holly rocked forward on her crutches. "Shaw, I'm not your normal witness. I've dealt with criminals before as an attorney. If anyone can get him to confess, I can."

Shaw bit off the tip of his fingernail and spit it into

the garbage. "All right. But we will be watching from behind the glass. Caleb has handcuffs on, but after the day I've had, I know not to trust them." His gaze slid toward Preston.

Preston shrugged. What could he say?

"You may feel as if you're alone with Caleb, but you won't be."

Holly peeked Preston's way. "I know."

Holly had dealt with many criminals before, just not any who had previously tried to kill her. She gripped her crutch handles tightly and waited for Shaw to open the door.

Preston had to remain in his handcuffs in the first interrogation room. His freedom depended on her success.

"You ready?" Shaw asked.

Was she? No. But God was. She nodded.

Shaw swung the door open. Holly took a deep breath and poked her crutches through the doorway so she could swing in after them. She planted her good foot.

Caleb's mouth dropped open. He leaned away.

The door snapped shut behind her. Last time she had been alone with this man, he'd been holding her head below water. But she couldn't mention that now. She couldn't lead the witness.

So she stood. She waited on God.

"Holly." Fear contorted Caleb's expression between attempts to act natural. He was probably reeling through excuses to find the best one for the occasion. He didn't sound as thankful she was alive as he had the first time they'd been questioned by police. How had she ever fallen for that act?

"Caleb," she greeted him in return. "May I join you?"

His eyes narrowed. He pressed his lips together. It had

to be killing him that he couldn't threaten her to keep quiet the way he'd threatened the security guard. He twitched. Rocked. Finally motioned for the seat across from him.

She hobbled forward. "Thank you."

"What are you doing here?"

She lowered herself to the chair and leaned her crutches on the floor. "I'm getting set up for the Witness Security Program."

He slammed his hands down on the table. His hand-cuffs jingled.

Holly tensed. She reached for a crutch to use as a weapon to defend herself. Yes, the police were only a few feet away, but after getting shot and having her femur cracked, she wasn't going to take any more chances.

Caleb cleared his throat and sat back as if the outburst had never happened. "You think Preston is going to keep trying to kill you?" he asked. "That makes me so angry."

She exhaled a breath she hadn't realized she'd been holding. Caleb was still putting on the show. "*That's* why you're angry?" she challenged him.

"Yes." He waved his arms with as much melodrama as the handcuffs would allow. This was the Caleb she knew. The one who got away with murder. "I thought he was on your side, but I guess he was jealous you agreed to marry me."

Her pulse raged at his overt lie, but what had she expected? He'd turned the tables like he always did. She needed to keep cool. She knew the truth no matter what he said.

"Perhaps."

"Well, I hope you are honest about it when you testify at his court case."

She wanted to throw her head back and laugh at his outlandish advice. But the joke was on her. If Caleb could keep a straight face through such an act, there was no way she was going to get him to crack.

She rose and situated the crutches beneath her arms. She was exhausted and in pain. No need to waste any more time with the manipulator when Preston was right next door and she'd have to leave him soon. "I can promise you I'll be honest when I speak to a jury. Whoever tried to kill me will be going to jail for a long, long time."

Caleb stilled as he watched her hobble a step forward. "How did you survive?"

She stopped. Turned her head to face him. She'd survived a lot of his attacks, but he must have been referring to the attempted drowning. "Did you forget I swam in college?"

His eyes burned with a new awareness. If she beat him here, she could do it again in court. He spoke slowly. "You...played...dead?"

She smiled sweetly. "Make no mistake, I outsmarted the killer."

He leaped to his feet and lunged for her.

She shifted her weight to lift the crutch as she'd planned to, but she was too unstable and the weapon too long to stop him.

He lifted his hands and brought them down with the cold chain tight around her neck. He pinned her back to his chest.

Her scream caught in her throat. The steel squeezed against her flesh. She reached for it with both hands to open the airway. Crutches dropped to the floor. She stepped down on her bad leg. The shooting pain muddled all sensations. Black spots blurred her vision.

The door slammed open. An array of cop uniforms appeared before her eyes as if she were looking through a kaleidoscope.

Shouting.

The grip on her throat slackened. Handcuffs scraped against her cheekbones and nose as Caleb was forced to release her. His knee bumped her as he tried for one more desperate escape, and then his chest gave way to thin air.

She kept her left leg lifted and reached for anything that might prevent her from tipping over into the commotion. Nothing steady. Then both feet were whisked out from underneath her.

Preston scooped her up and hugged her to his solid chest. "Wanna get out of here, doll?" he asked.

She looked down at the hands that held her, wrists still cuffed together. There was nothing that would keep this man from rescuing her. She twisted to face him and wrap her arms around him in return. "I'll stay here with you as long as I have to."

His eyes roamed her face. "Thanks to you, that's not going to be very long."

Sure enough, Shaw finished up reading Caleb his rights and turned to face the couple. "It's been a long two days, but it looks like this little lady's prayers have been answered. You've earned your freedom, Tyler. Not that these things ever stopped you from anything." He shot Holly a wry smile as he twisted his key to loosen Preston's bonds.

Holly sighed in satisfaction. Caleb's attempt to choke her had given Preston the freedom she'd been praying for. And she was finally free to be his doll again.

Preston carried a sleeping Holly through the front door of his cabin. With as long as they'd had to spend at the police station, the sun was coming up and both sets of their parents were due to arrive at any time. It would be a reunion to remember, but if he and Holly were going to pick up where they'd left off four years before, he needed to make things right between them.

He lowered her gently to the couch and brushed hair back from her face. Should he wake her up or let her rest?

He'd let her rest. She'd been through so much. He'd just practice his apology on her sleeping form. "I'm sorry I ever let you think I died, Holly."

Her eyelids fluttered open. She quietly studied his face.

Practice time was over. He knelt on his knees in front of her. "I realize how wrong that was. When I thought you were dead tonight…" His voice trailed away as tears pooled in his eyes. There were no words for the pain of mourning.

She lifted a palm to his cheek. "It's okay."

He leaned into her touch. "It is now, but it wasn't. You were right about my fear keeping me from loving you the way I should have."

She bit her lip. "And I'm sorry about agreeing to marry Caleb out of loneliness. If you can forgive me for that, I can forgive you for anything."

He examined the pink area of her neck where Caleb had choked her. It would probably be sore for a few days. "You saved my life, Holly."

She reached for his fingers and entwined them with hers. "You saved mine."

He ran his thumb over the back of her hand. They could argue all night about who'd saved who. Or he could just quote the scripture she'd been trying to pound into his thick skull. "'Two are better than one.'"

She gave a soft smile. "Though I was never alone, I was lonely without you."

He kissed her nose. "If I have anything to say about it, you are never going to be lonely again."

She lifted her chin to catch a second kiss on her lips.

"I'm really glad I serve a God who can bring the dead back to life."

What had she said? The warmth of her lips and softness of the touch momentarily turned his brain to static. Something about how God restored lives? Well, he wasn't going to waste one more minute of his. He scrambled to his feet and climbed the ladder to the loft.

"Preston?" She lifted to her elbows.

He pulled his gaze away from her to hunt down the ring. There on the shelf, where he'd put it all those years before. Preston snatched the small velvet box, his insides doing somersaults in anticipation. Was he being hasty? Not at all. If anything, his proposal was overdue. He scaled back down the rungs.

She cocked her head. "What are you doing?"

He dropped back to his knees and snapped the box open. "Doll, if I'm going to come back to life, it's going to be so I can spend the rest of it with you. I love you, Holly Fontaine. I have since you shoved me off the dock for scaring you with a firecracker."

Her cheeks ripened. Her eyes glistened. "And I've loved you since you put that frog in my favorite pair of flats."

Really? Because he'd hoped she'd forgotten about that. But if she was going to love him, it was sometimes going to have to be in spite of him.

"I did that because I was afraid to kiss you. I guess I've always been afraid of love. But I'm not anymore." He pulled the simple solitaire free to sparkle in the lamplight. "Holly Fontaine, will you marry me?"

"Oh yes." She slipped her finger into the perfect circle and wiggled her eyebrows. "And so you know, that Fourth of July stunt wasn't the first time I felt fireworks around you."

Preston couldn't stop smiling as he lowered his head

toward hers to seal their commitment with a kiss. Softening his heart to Holly had allowed him to hurt more, but in the end it also brought the healing he needed. He'd never been more alive.

* * * * *

*If you enjoyed PRESUMED DEAD
by Angela Ruth Strong,
look for these other reunion romance stories
from Love Inspired Suspense:*

*DEADLY SETUP by Annslee Urban
HIGH-RISK REUNION by Margaret Daley
ABDUCTED by Dana Mentink
HIGH SPEED HOLIDAY by Katy Lee
HAZARDOUS HOLIDAY by Liz Johnson
MISTLETOE REUNION THREAT by Virginia Vaughan*

Dear Reader,

I had so much fun researching this story. SOAR and the CID are real. The locations on Lake Tahoe are real—including the secret tunnel. And even the flaws in the characters are real. But I didn't have to research those.

See, I'm like Holly in the way that I lost a relationship that I thought would last forever, and I was terrified of being alone. It would have been very easy for me to make the same mistake Holly made in committing to the wrong person. So often, as women, we want the romance. We want to feel desired. And so we compromise our relationship with Christ to have a relationship we tell ourselves God wants for us because it will make us happy. But, as Holly found out, true happiness didn't come from being loved. It came from loving—even when the man she loved made it very clear there was no future for them together.

Preston was that man. He was the exact opposite of Holly. He'd lost so many people he loved that he didn't ever want to love again. And he figured God felt the same way toward him. He believed he was doing the right thing by pushing Holly away, and it took almost losing her to realize love was worth fighting for. This is similar to where my husband was at when I met him. Jim was planning to move to Alaska and write off women for good. But God had better plans. Just like God always does.

The Bible says two are better than one. This doesn't have to mean romantic relationships. It means we are created for community. We are created to learn and grow together with Him.

In the end, Holly and Preston learned this lesson from each other. The same way I got to learn this lesson along with my real-life hero. Jim is the reason I'm able to write about romance again. Love changes lives, which changes the world. And there's nothing else I'd rather write about.

This is my first book with Love Inspired Suspense, and I'm thrilled you chose to read it. It hasn't been easy, but just like Holly and Preston became stronger when working together, I am a better writer because of working with my editor. I hope I keep getting better, and I hope you'll join me on the journey. Please stop by for a visit at www.angelaruthstrong.com, and always feel free to share your story with me at: angelaruthstrong@gmail.com.

Love always,
Angela

COMING NEXT MONTH FROM
Love Inspired® Suspense

Available March 7, 2017

MISTAKEN IDENTITY
Mission: Rescue • by Shirlee McCoy

When Trinity Miller's attacked by a man who believes she's Mason Gains's girlfriend, the former army pilot turned reclusive prosthetic maker is forced from seclusion to rescue her. But the assailant won't stop targeting her—unless Mason gives up information on one of his clients.

HER BABY'S PROTECTOR
by Margaret Daley and Susan Sleeman

As babies are thrust into danger in two brand-new novellas, these men will stop at nothing to keep them—and their lovely single mothers—safe.

PLAIN SANCTUARY • by Alison Stone

Running her new Amish community bed-and-breakfast, Heather Miller believes she's finally safe from her violent ex-husband—until he escapes from prison to come after her. Now her only hope of survival is relying on US Marshal Zach Walker for protection.

THE SEAL'S SECRET CHILD
Navy SEAL Defenders • by Elisabeth Rees

When former SEAL Edward "Blade" Harding receives an email from his six-year-old son, he's shocked—both by the news that he has a child and by his son's message. Someone's threatening to kill Blade's ex-fiancée, defense attorney Josie Bishop...and she and their little boy need his help.

SECURITY DETAIL
Secret Service Agents • by Lisa Phillips

A mobster is after the former president's daughter Kayla Harris, and she's not sure why. But undercover Secret Service agent Conner Thorne's determined to find out...and save her life.

OUTSIDE THE LAW • by Michelle Karl

Former military recruit Yasmine Browder plans to uncover the truth about her brother's death...but her investigation quickly turns deadly. And her childhood friend rookie FBI agent Noel Black risks his career—and his life—to help her solve the mystery.

———————

LISCNM0217

REQUEST YOUR FREE BOOKS!
2 FREE RIVETING INSPIRATIONAL NOVELS
PLUS 2 FREE MYSTERY GIFTS

Love Inspired.
SUSPENSE
RIVETING INSPIRATIONAL ROMANCE

YES! Please send me 2 FREE Love Inspired® Suspense novels and my 2 FREE mystery gifts (gifts are worth about $10). After receiving them, if I don't wish to receive any more books, I can return the shipping statement marked "cancel." If I don't cancel, I will receive 4 brand-new novels every month and be billed just $4.99 per book in the U.S. or $5.49 per book in Canada. That's a savings of at least 17% off the cover price. It's quite a bargain! Shipping and handling is just 50¢ per book in the U.S. and 75¢ per book in Canada.* I understand that accepting the 2 free books and gifts places me under no obligation to buy anything. I can always return a shipment and cancel at any time. Even if I never buy another book, the two free books and gifts are mine to keep forever.

123/323 IDN GH5Z

Name _____ (PLEASE PRINT)

Address _____ Apt. #

City _____ State/Prov. _____ Zip/Postal Code

Signature (if under 18, a parent or guardian must sign)

Mail to the **Reader Service:**
IN U.S.A.: P.O. Box 1867, Buffalo, NY 14240-1867
IN CANADA: P.O. Box 609, Fort Erie, Ontario L2A 5X3

Are you a current subscriber to Love Inspired® Suspense books and want to receive the larger-print edition?
Call 1-800-873-8635 or visit www.ReaderService.com.

* Terms and prices subject to change without notice. Prices do not include applicable taxes. Sales tax applicable in N.Y. Canadian residents will be charged applicable taxes. Offer not valid in Quebec. This offer is limited to one order per household. Not valid for current subscribers to Love Inspired Suspense books. All orders subject to credit approval. Credit or debit balances in a customer's account(s) may be offset by any other outstanding balance owed by or to the customer. Please allow 4 to 6 weeks for delivery. Offer available while quantities last.

Your Privacy—The Reader Service is committed to protecting your privacy. Our Privacy Policy is available online at www.ReaderService.com or upon request from the Reader Service.
We make a portion of our mailing list available to reputable third parties that offer products we believe may interest you. If you prefer that we not exchange your name with third parties, or if you wish to clarify or modify your communication preferences, please visit us at www.ReaderService.com/consumerschoice or write to us at Reader Service Preference Service, P.O. Box 9062, Buffalo, NY 14240-9062. Include your complete name and address.

LIS15

Mason scanned the lake, then the trees behind them. "I
don't like the feel of things. You have your phone?"

"Yes." Trinity fished it out of her pocket.

"Text your brother. Tell him to meet us down here—and
to come armed."

She texted quickly, her fingers shaking with adrenaline
and fear.

Chance texted back immediately and she tucked the
phone away again. "He and Cyrus are on the way. He said
to stay where we are."

"Where we are makes us sitting ducks." He stood,
pulling her to her feet. "They want you, Trinity. I've got
no doubt about that. They think they can use you as a pawn
to get what they want from me."

"You're assuming someone is here. It's possible—"

The crack of gunfire split the air and she was on the
ground, Mason covering her, her body pressed into the

damp sand. She thought she heard an engine, but she couldn't hear much past the blood pulsing in her ears.

"Listen to me," Mason said, his mouth close to her ear. "They're coming down on mopeds. That's going to make it nearly impossible for them to get a clean shot. We've got to make it to the canoe and we've got to make it there quickly. You ready to run?"

She nodded because she couldn't get enough air in her lungs to speak. And then he was up, yanking her to her feet again, sprinting across the beach, the sound of pursuit growing louder behind them.

Mason pulled his knife from its ankle sheath, slashing the rope that held his boat to the spindly bushes that grew near the water's edge.

"Get in," he yelled, holding Trinity's arm as she hopped into the aluminum hull. He followed quickly, shoving away from the shore, moving them out into deeper water as quickly as he could. As soon as he was clear, he prepped the outboard motor, his eyes on the woods.

They weren't out of gunshot range yet. Not even close.

Don't miss
MISTAKEN IDENTITY by Shirlee McCoy,
available March 2017 wherever
Love Inspired® Suspense books and ebooks are sold.

www.LoveInspired.com

*Can an Amish teacher find love with the Amish fireman
down the road, or will her secret force them apart?*

Read on for a sneak preview of
HIS AMISH TEACHER,
the next book in **Patricia Davids**'s
heartwarming series, **AMISH BACHELORS**.

"We all know Teacher Lillian is a terrible cook, don't we,
children?"

Lillian Keim's students erupted into giggles and some
outright laughter. She crossed her arms and pressed her
lips together to hold back a smile.

Timothy Bowman winked at her to take any sting out
of his comment, but she wasn't offended. They had been
friends for ages and were members of the same Amish
community in Bowmans Crossing, Ohio. She knew he
enjoyed a good joke as well as the next fellow, but he
was deadly serious about his job today and so was she.
The lessons they were presenting might one day prevent
a tragedy.

He stood in front of her class on the infield of the softball
diamond behind the one-room Amish schoolhouse where
she taught all eight grades. Dressed in full fireman's
turnout gear, Timothy made an impressive figure. The
coat and pants added bulk to his slender frame, but he
carried the additional weight with ease. His curly brown

hair was hidden under a yellow helmet instead of his usual straw hat, but his hazel eyes sparkled with mirth. A smile lifted one side of his mouth and deepened the dimples in his tanned cheeks. Timothy smiled a lot. It was one reason she liked him.

His bulky fire coat and pants with bright fluorescent yellow banding weren't Plain clothing, but their Amish church district approved their use because the church elders and the bishop recognized the need for Amish volunteers to help fill the ranks of the local non-Amish fire company. The county fire marshal understood the necessity of special education in the Amish community, where open flames and gas lanterns were used regularly. The Amish didn't allow electricity in their homes. Biannual fire-safety classes were held at all the local Amish schools. This was Timothy's first time giving the class. With Lillian's permission, he was deviating from the normal script with a demonstration outside. Timothy wanted to make an impression on the children. She admired that.

Don't miss
HIS AMISH TEACHER by Patricia Davids,
available March 2017 wherever
Love Inspired® books and ebooks are sold.

www.LoveInspired.com

LIEXP0217